This
IS ME

This
IS ME

SHANELL W. WILKES

CHAPTER
ONE

Released Me

I had been sitting in my office, listening to my favorite song, "I Am Changing" by Jareennifer Hudson, from the soundtrack of *Dream Girls*. Actually, I hadn't just been sitting, I had been pacing, too. Pacing, sitting, and tapping—my husband's pet peeves. He knew I did those things when I had a lot on my mind, *or* when I had a lot I needed to get off my mind, a lot I needed to release.

I loved "I Am Changing" from the moment I first heard it. It described me perfectly. It had been what I wanted and needed for my life: a change. The lyrics had given me hope. They released me. They made me feel free and whole; they allowed me to breathe. Sometimes, I felt the song had been written just for me. I wanted change in my life. I needed to change, but that was easier said than done. Tears began to slide down my face. Like Jennifer Hudson's character in the film, I had spent so much of my life in darkness, which made me blind to things I should have noticed.

I knew the song had not been written for me because no one truly knew what I had gone through. I never let anyone in. Not my two childhood best friends. Not my caring grandma. Not even my devoted, loving husband. I had never allowed my hurt, disappointments, betrayals, or brokenness to show; sadly, I had almost become void of any emotion.

"Buzz, buzz!" The sound scared me from my trance.

"Yes?" I spoke into the intercom.

"Your nine o'clock is here, Dr. O'Brien," my assistant responded.

"Damn!" I had thought to myself. "Right on time. Hell, she better be, with all this damn money I'm paying her."

"Thanks, Nikki!" I responded. "Send her right up. Nikki, thanks again for coming in on a Saturday just to greet this appointment for me. I don't know what I would have done without you. I owe you big time!"

Nikki said, "Dr. O'Brien, you don't owe me a thing. You giving me this job has been thanks enough, not to mention what was inside the envelope I found on my desk this morning. I don't have to tell you that it was way too much because you already know that."

I smiled. I loved making my employees happy.

"Nikki, once my client steps on the elevator, be sure to lock up, and have an amazing day!"

"Will do!" she assured me.

I inhaled deeply, then exhaled. I recited the phrase Grandma recited to me all my life.

"Cherry, you have survived too many storms to be bothered by raindrops."

I stood. I checked my reflection in the mirror to ensure that there had been no trace of the tear from earlier. I touched up my lipstick. I straightened my back and stood with the seed of confidence Grandma planted in me decades ago. I tugged slightly at my Tom Ford short, peplum jacket; then I traipsed over to the door, somewhat unsure of myself, to greet my client. I began to wonder if I had been the client instead!

Nothing in the world could have prepared me for that moment. Opening the door had been like opening that black hole that had been buried deep inside my soul. I greeted my guest, then offered her a seat. I pressed a button to silence my theme song, closed my office door, and sat down. I looked at her. She looked at me. I tapped my nails on my desk. She crossed her legs. I straightened my back again, readjusted my suit, and then locked eyes with hers. Our gazes had been fixed. I dared her to speak. She seemed to do the same to me. A smile found the corner of my mouth, but I kept it hidden. She broke her gaze. Finally, I spoke.

"I am usually really good at reading people, but I find you quite the challenge."

The look in her eyes told me that she took this as a compliment.

I continued, "But, I guess, today, you are here to read me!"

She spoke for the first time. "Thanks for choosing me to see you today, Dr. O'Brien."

"Well, that confirms it. I guess I am the client," I think to myself.

That time, the smile in the corner of my mouth escaped.

I respond, "Most importantly, thank you for agreeing to come under my terms, which includes devoting your entire 9 to 5 to me."

Still, her eyes had been locked on mine.

"My assistant has prepared chilled beverages and a charcuterie board. The ladies' room is through those double doors. Here is a beautiful view overlooking Los Angeles. If there is anything else you need, just let me know."

The inevitable, inherited sassiness from Grandma provoked me to stand to my feet, cross my arms, lock eyes with hers once again and say, "Dr. Sartori, as I mentioned at your arrival, I find it quite difficult to read what you are thinking, so I'll give it a go. You are shocked at the figure that stands before you, most people are. They assume that the brains behind this billion-dollar empire is a man, a White one at that. But see, like them, you are wrong. I built this shit. I am the brains behind this company. It was me who made this happen. A woman; an educated, beautiful, black woman at that."

She seemed unmoved by my words. She leaned in a little closer, then spoke again for the second time since her arrival.

"Dr. O'Brien, you are wrong. I know exactly who you are. See, I've done my research, too. I am simply curious as to what this meeting is about. As you already know, I am a busy woman with many, important, high-powered clients, none of whom have ever requested my services in the manner you have. One, my clients always come to me. Two, they only get 60 minutes of my time each visit. So, when you requested that I come to you instead and that this would be a one-time, all-day appointment, I assumed that this is a life-or-death situation. Three, just so you know, I built my shit, too, because I, too, am a woman, an educated, beautiful woman of color."

At that, I took my seat. We had both let a smile slip out. That was when I knew that Dr. Sartori had been the only person who could possibly help me. She had been the only one who could release me.

CHAPTER
TWO

Changed Me

Growing up, I thought I had a normal childhood: Momma, Daddy, my two older brothers, a dog, and a goldfish. In my mind, I had the perfect family. As early as the age of three, I remembered my parents instilling love, respect, education, and God in the lives of my brothers and me. Momma had taken us to church four days each week: Mondays for prayer service, Wednesdays for Bible study, Fridays for choir practice, and Sundays for regular service. We had been taught to say yes ma'am and yes sir to our elders. Our parents had been highly involved in our education, so we excelled academically.

Momma had been gorgeous. Her name was Grace. I could immediately pull her beauty to the forefront of my memory. Back then, she was five feet, eight inches tall and weighed 175 pounds. She had been thick in all the right places, with wavy, black hair just past her shoulders. Her skin was dark mocha, with beautiful brown eyes, and perfectly white teeth to match. She worked a regular 9 to 5 as a receptionist at a local doctor's office, and she always had dinner on the table by 6:30.

Daddy's looks matched Momma's. His name was William. He had chocolate skin, brown eyes, and white teeth, too. He sported a salt-and-pepper beard, had the body of a muscular god, and always dressed in tailored suits. Growing up, Daddy worked just as hard as Momma, so we had not seen him much. I had never been sure what he did for a living, but he had always made it home to tuck me in at night. However, he had always been gone in the mornings no matter how early I woke up to see him off.

Both of my brothers were older than me. Greyson was five years older than me; Sterling was only fourteen months younger than Greyson. I guessed my parents had a thing for naming their children after colors because they named me Cherry, although most people called me Riri or Missy. Both of my brothers looked like younger versions of Daddy. They were my protectors. They loved me just as much as they loved football, and football had been their life. We had done everything together: football, fishing, biking, football, tea parties, football, dolls, teachers, football, hide-and-seek, and football. They read to me, prayed with me, and had always taken care of me when Momma and Daddy had been at work. My family had not been rich by any means, but we had a lovely home, two nice cars, and all the things we needed and most of the things we wanted.

The family I had known and loved changed when I was ten. I'll never forget the day. It had been a Thursday evening.

Momma, my brothers, and I had been doing our weekly shopping at the local supermarket. Our cart was piled high with all the things we needed for the week. Momma had even let each of us pick out our own box of cereal, bags of potato chips, bottles of juice, and chocolate candy. We were heading for the checkout when it happened. I had seen Daddy.

With excitement, I yelled, "Daddyyyy!"

I started running towards him. Just before I reached him, Greyson and Sterling grabbed me by my arms. Daddy was with some woman and little girl that I had never seen before. Daddy grabbed the woman and little girl by the hands and turned away as if he did not hear me or even know me.

I started screaming and crying and tried pulling away from my brothers.

I yelled at the top of my lungs, "Let me go. I want my daddy. What's wrong with y'all? Let me go! Daddy, Daddyyyy!"

By that time, everyone in the supermarket was looking at me.

Daddy sped up. The woman and little girl just stared at me like I was crazy. Leaving our shopping cart behind, Momma and my brothers carried me, kicking and screaming, all the way to our car.

They stuffed me into the car and jumped in. Momma pulled off before the car doors were closed all the way. I yelled and screamed all the way home. Momma, Greyson, and Sterling remained silent. Once we got home, I ran straight to my bedroom and slammed the door. I was flabbergasted and had several questions. Why did we leave the store like that? Why did Daddy look at me like he didn't know me? Why didn't he run to me, pick me up, and twirl me around, like he always does? Why wouldn't Greyson and Sterling let me run to him? Who was that little girl? Who was that woman? Why did we leave all our groceries? Why were Momma and my brothers so quiet in the car? The answers to all those questions came about two hours later.

I cried myself to sleep. A knock at my door scared me out of the nightmare I thought I was having.

Momma whispered, "Missy, we need to talk."

I did not respond. I was furious. Slowly, she opened my bedroom door. Momma, Greyson, and Sterling tiptoed into my room and joined me on my bed. I looked at them through swollen, red, teary eyes. It seemed as if they had been crying too. We sat in silence for a few minutes. I felt nervous. I could tell something wasn't right.

Momma finally spoke. "I have something to tell you, Missy. It's something that we've been keeping from you for a very long time. Your daddy and I shared it with your brothers when they were a little younger than you. It was difficult for us to tell them and even more difficult for me to tell you now. We all agreed to tell you when the time was right, but it never felt right."

I sat up in bed. I will never forget the hurt Momma and my brothers had on their faces. I couldn't imagine what they were about to tell me. Nothing could have ever prepared me for what Momma said next.

"Missy," Momma continued, "first, we all love you very much and that will never change. This is the reason it's so hard for me to tell you this. We've been keeping a terrible secret from you. A painful one. A secret that could destroy the lives of so many people."

I noticed my older brother, Greyson, twisting his fingers together. To this day, he still does this when he is nervous.

Sterling cleared his throat and said, "Missy, don't get mad at Momma. It's not her fault."

I started crying again. I searched everyone's face for a clue as to what the secret may have been. All I saw were tears, hurt, and shame.

Momma grabbed both of my hands, looked down at the floor and said, "Missy, those people we saw in the supermarket with your daddy are his wife and daughter. We.... we are his secret family."

I will never forget the three words that came out of my mouth next. I heard them on TV, the playground, in the neighborhood, and at school, but never in my own home.

I screamed, "What the fuck?!?"

Dr. Sartori looked up from her pad and pen. She seemed to be just as shocked today as I had been so many years ago when Momma revealed the secret.

She said, "Excuse me?"

I said, "That's right. That SOB was married, which explained why he was never home when I woke up each morning. On the other hand, it left me with so many questions. The main ones being, how could Momma be so damn stupid, and how could my brothers keep or, should I say, be so understanding of the secret?"

"Nevertheless, the secret destroyed my relationship with Momma, my brothers, and Daddy. I never could forgive them for it. I couldn't trust them. I didn't even know them. I couldn't even look at them the same. I cried for hours that night. Those hours turned into days. Those days turned into weeks, and those weeks turned into months. I stopped talking to everyone, and I stayed in my room most of the time. I barely ate. They begged me to 'snap out of it'. But it wasn't just an 'It'." That secret changed everything. My life changed. My respect for them changed. The ones I valued and respected most, did not reciprocate the same respect. Even though I was young, I had an idea what that meant. Momma and Daddy were liars and did not value marriage. I started to question my entire world. Was all the time we spent in church a lie? Were they all hypo-crites? Could they be trusted? They bought me gifts and tried to act like nothing changed. But it only made me hate them more. They destroyed my world. They changed me."

CHAPTER
THREE

Saved Me

Eventually, my maternal grandma intervened. She traveled to New York and moved me to Texas to live with her. Although it broke Momma's heart, it was the best choice for my mental and emotional well-being. Even at that young age, I understood that she had saved me. With her abundant love and patience, my healing journey began.

Dr. Sartori rested her left hand under her left cheekbone and asked, "So, how can I help you?"

I answered, "That secret affected my entire life. It allowed people to use me in ways you would never imagine. In return, I learned to use, abuse, mistreat, and distrust people. I was so determined to not be like my parents and brothers that I was willing to do anything to prevent that. No one knows the things I have done or the things I allowed people to do to me on my journey to be different from Momma, Daddy, and Grey and Sterl."

Dr. Sartori interrupted, "Well, there is a possibility that I may be able to offer you my services and some support. But I'm not a miracle worker. You can't expect me to do that today in this one session. This kind of treatment and therapy takes months, sometimes years."

I interrupted her and said, "Well, you don't have months or years, and I don't need to be fixed or treated. I just need to get it out. Dr. Sartori, I have kept so many secrets. Secrets that have gotten me where I am today. Secrets that could destroy me. Honestly, these secrets are slowly killing me."

"Killing me" seemed to get her attention.

I continued, "Dr. Sartori, what I just told you is nothing. It's just the tip of the iceberg. There is so much more. I've done my research and found that you are the best. So, Dr. Sartori, you must save me from my secrets, myself, and my own destruction. I start my story and don't finish it, there's no telling what I will do. That's why you are here today, just to listen. This is my place of comfort. It's what I have worked so hard to achieve and why I did some of the terrible things I did."

I stopped talking because the tears started falling.

Dr. Sartori said, "Alright, I think I'm starting to understand a bit more. Before we get started, could you point me toward the ladies' room?"

I pointed, and she left the room.

After that, I fell to my knees and prayed.

"Dear God, I need You like I've never needed You before. You already know the things I have done, and You also know my heart. Lord, I come before You asking You for forgiveness. Forgive me for the things I have done, and the people I have hurt. Lord, I cry out to You for forgiveness. I cry out to You for help. Help me to forgive myself. Help me to tell my story. Help me to find the courage to move past the mistakes I've made and the sins I've committed. Lord, please give Dr. Sartori the ears to listen. Only You know what it is that I need from her. I pray that I leave this session today renewed and refreshed. I pray for change, Lord, that only You can give. Save me from myself. Dear Lord, I pray. Amen."

I recited, "Cherry, you have survived too many storms to be bothered by raindrops."

CHAPTER
FOUR

Comforted Me

At fourteen, I started high school and met Dr. Miller, our principal. I was still living with Grandma in Texas. Dr. Miller was an exceptional educator. He had been respected as a mentor and role model by the community. He knew each student by name, and he prioritized hiring the best teachers, understanding that their happiness was essential for student success. Because of his leadership, our school consistently ranked first in both local and state assessments. We thrived not only academically but also in sports like football, basketball, baseball, tennis, swimming, and any other activities we pursued.

Dr. Miller cultivated strong relationships with the community and parents, making it a privilege to be a student or staff member at his school. He held a well-deserved place of admiration. To me, he was the ideal person, embodying qualities I hoped for in a father figure. He was devoted to helping everyone, including me.

Sadly, things between us changed when I turned sixteen. Growing up, Grandam had always taught me about self-respect, dignity, and how to carry myself as a young lady. She taught me to protect and save my "honeypot," that what she called a woman's private area, for marriage.

She would always say, "Missy, your "honeypot" is one of your most valued possessions. Don't let anyone dip in it unless it is your husband."

Due to the pain, I'd felt from my family, I couldn't see the inner or outer beauty that Grandma and others saw in me. All I noticed was a dark-skinned, brown-eyed, flat-chested stick figure. But that all changed when I turned sixteen. I blossomed. My skin appeared silky, my eyes were the color of caramel, my chest filled out, and my waist remained small while my curves developed beautifully. My years of dance and gymnastics gave me poise, flexibility, and a graceful stride. I think I noticed my transformation just as others did.

I should also mention my two best friends, Summer and Aubrey, who lived just a few doors away from Grandma's house. Grandma had known them for years, having babysat them when they were younger, and she quickly introduced us. Over time, we became inseparable. Summer, an only child, was the most outgoing of the three of us. She stood about five-foot-three, weighed around 120 pounds, and had a beautiful brown complexion, curves, long hair extensions, and acrylic nails. Aubrey, though not shy, was quieter than Summer. She had a younger brother, stood about five-foot-seven, and weighed around 115 pounds. Being biracial, with a black father and white mother, her complexion resembled her father's. She had long, natural black hair with waves. While Aubrey wasn't as curvy, she was beautiful in her own way, both inside and out.

Meeting Summer and Aubrey was exactly what I needed to replace the bond I'd lost with Greyson and Sterling, a fact that Grandma understood when she introduced us. At first, I wanted nothing to do with them. But they visited Grandma's house daily, bringing their laughter and warmth into the family room. At first, I pretended they weren't there, but gradually, I found myself looking forward to their visits. We shared the same schools, from elementary to high school, and their presence marked the beginning of a healing process for me. Though I didn't reveal what had happened in New York, their companionship brought me comfort and strength. Over time, I began to like—and even trust—them.

During our junior year of high school, we performed in the school's talent show, an idea Summer came up with. We chose to perform Destiny's Child's "Bills, Bills, Bills"—our favorite song. Summer took on Beyoncé's role, Aubrey was Michelle, and I was Kelly. Every spare moment we had, we practiced together. Our outfits, inspired by those in the music video, were pink, black, and white, hugging our bodies and accentuating our shapes. They had cutouts that revealed just enough to make us feel daring.

On the day of the show, we stepped on stage to an unexpected silence—the DJ hadn't even started the music. It felt like we'd entered the Twilight Zone. Scanning the audience, I met Grandma's eyes, and a wave of embarrassment hit me. I tried to cover myself with my arms, and after a quick exchange of glances, the three of us decided to leave the stage.

Suddenly, someone shouted, "Got damn!"

Instantly, others joined in and the whistling, cheering, and clapping began. The music started, and we jolted to our starting positions.

Our performance was magical. We sang and danced like we owned the song. The cheering, clapping, and whistling kept coming. When we were done, we were high with excitement. There was no doubt in our minds that we would take first place. At the end when the MC announced us as the winners, the room erupted with excitement. We felt famous as hell. Some of our peers even asked for our autographs, which pumped us up a little more.

On our drive home, I was talking a mile a minute.

"Grandma, I'm a star. This must be what it feels like to be Destiny's Child for real. Maybe, we should go somewhere to audition."

Grandma remained silent, which meant something was wrong. She was not celebrating with me.

"Grandma, what's wrong?" I asked.

She took a deep breath and said, "Missy."

I knew it was going to be a serious talk because she didn't say, "Missy," using that tone, unless it was something serious.

"You're a beautiful young lady. You're intelligent and have such greatness coming your way. Girl, God, has a plan for you that will blow your mind. But remember, you must stay in His will. You don't have to use your body to open the eyes, minds, ears, and mouths of the people around you. With His guidance, your works will open those things. Girl, you will move mountains."

I was quiet for the rest of the ride home. I couldn't believe Grandma had ruined the moment with one of her lectures. I bet Summer and Aubrey's parents didn't give them a lecture. I didn't say anything else to Grandma for the rest of the night. In fact, I don't think Grandma and I ever mentioned the talent show again.

When my friends and I showed up at school that Monday, it was like we'd become instant celebrities. Everyone was talking about us—boys wanted to date us, and the girls couldn't help but feel a bit of envy. One guy, in particular, seemed to be watching me every chance he got. At first, I thought I was imagining it. You know that feeling when you sense someone's watching you. But he made sure I knew it wasn't just a feeling. He was intentional, and I could feel his gaze. When I'd look back, he'd meet my eyes and hold the stare, daring me to look away first, which I always did. He'd been at the talent show that night and started showing up at school, afterwards.

It was Braylen Miller—Dr. Miller's son. He'd come around school occasionally. As a student at the local university, he'd often drop by to visit his dad. But after that night, it seemed like he was hanging around more. I'd noticed him before because of how respectful he was toward his dad and other adults at school. And as if that wasn't enough, he looked just as good as he acted. Braylen was seriously handsome, like a modern-day Fresh Prince but with even more swagger.

He had jet-black, wavy hair, dark, intriguing eyes, a perfect smile with straight, white teeth, and smooth milk-chocolate skin. Tall and well-built, his clothes showed off his sinewy frame in just the right way. His hands were large, strong, and well-kept.

When he visited, he'd usually be in athletic shorts, his fraternity T-shirt, and boots or sneakers. Occasionally, he'd show up in custom-fitted slacks and a dress shirt. My friends and I couldn't get enough of him. And honestly, who could blame us?

I spent a lot of time at school after hours. I was involved in so much—National Beta Club, varsity cheerleading, debate team, class president, office assistant, academic challenge captain, president of both the Spanish Club and Beta Club, and a member of the volleyball and softball teams, to name a few. These activities gave me plenty of chances to see Braylen when he was at school.

I remember the conversation with my best friends as if it happened yesterday.

I said, "Aubrey, I think Braylen is checking me out."

Summer rolled her eyes and interjected, "Girl please. He don't want you. He got his hands full with college girls. Why would he waste his time eyeing you?"

Aubrey said, "Hell, everybody's been checking us out since the talent show, so I wouldn't doubt it. We are the hottest things walking the halls of South High School."

Summer and Aubrey continued talking, laughing, and joking around, but my mind drifted off. I couldn't help but wonder if it was all in my head, or if Dr. Miller's son was really eyeing me. I got my answer the next day.

Summer, Aubrey, and I were leaving volleyball practice when I realized I'd left my duffel bag on the bleachers. I said goodbye to them and headed back to the gym. As I was walking, I spotted Braylen getting out of his car, looking fine in Nike shorts, his fraternity shirt, and sneakers. I figured he was there to shoot some hoops. Then came that familiar stare, and I started to feel a little uneasy. I hurried into the school, grabbed my bag, and slung the strap over my shoulder.

I walked a bit slower on the way back, hoping he'd be out of sight by the time I reached the exit.

I got to the doors, there he was, standing there like he'd been waiting. My cheeks began to warm, and my palms felt clammy. I was about to push the door open when he stepped forward and held it open for me.

I stepped out and said, "Thanks so much."

He smiled and said, "Totally my pleasure. Let me help you with your bag."

Before I could protest, he had already taken it off my shoulder. We walked to my car in silence. I felt uneasy, wondering if I'd imagined the whole "checking me out" thing. Maybe he was simply being the gentleman his parents had raised him to be and was showing the same courtesy his father showed daily. That thought helped me relax a little. I opened the back door, and he gently placed my bag inside.

As I reached for the driver's door, he gently stopped me, smiled, and said, "A lady should never open her own car door when there's a gentleman around."

I couldn't help but smile back at him, and I thanked him for walking me to my car. As I got in and reached for my seatbelt, he gently took my left hand, brushed it with his soft, warm lips. He placed a tender kiss on it, sending chills through me like nothing I'd ever felt before. Lost in that moment, still smiling, I closed my eyes.

He chuckled and said, "I would love to see you smile like that more often. It looks amazing on you."

After that, he gave me a small piece of paper and said, "You should call me sometimes. We can get to know each other a little better."

He leaned into the car, took hold of my seatbelt, stretched it across me, and buckled it. We were just inches apart, and he smelled so damn good. As he clicked the seatbelt, his cheek lightly brushed against mine, bringing back those chills. This time, I tried to ignore them. Without saying another word, he closed my door and walked away. I couldn't help but wonder if he could feel me watching him as he left.

Summer and Aubrey called me as soon as I started my car. I didn't tell them what happened because I couldn't risk the chance of them telling me it was all in my head, again. A part of me felt bad because we shared everything with each other. I couldn't remember driving home or what we talked about because my mind was still on Braylen.

When I got out of my car, the small piece of paper that Braylen gave me fell to the ground. I picked it up and carefully unfolded it. His number was written on it. Was this some type of joke? Was Braylen really trying to get with me? Too afraid to find out, I folded the piece of paper and stuffed it in my purse and bounced into the house.

"Hey Grandma" I yelled, "something smells great."

"I'm in the kitchen Missy; dinner is almost ready. How was school?" she called out.

"Grandma," I said, "it was perfect."

"Well, tell me about it."

I tried to suppress my smile, knowing I couldn't share with Grandma what had made my day so perfect.

Instead, I said, "I got an A on my pre-calculus test."

She said, "Congratulations Missy! I knew you could do it. I told you that you have greatness in front of you! God is good."

"All the time!" I responded.

I felt a little bad about lying. Well, I didn't lie, but I didn't tell her the real reason I was wearing that smile.

A few days went by, and I tried to push thoughts of Braylen out of my mind. Not seeing him around after school made it easier, and I'd even forgotten about the slip of paper he'd given me. On Friday afternoon, I decided to treat myself to a latte at the drive-thru of the local coffee shop. It had been a long week, and I needed a moment to relax. We'd already cheered at two basketball games, with another one that night. But I didn't mind Friday night games—they were always a blast. The latte was just the pick-me-up I needed to get through it.

As I reached into my purse for cash, Braylen's slip of paper fell out again. Why did it keep resurfacing? Was this a sign?

After that, I couldn't stop thinking about him. I expected to see him at the game, but he was nowhere around. I even pretended to casually stop by Dr. Miller's office, hoping to catch a glimpse of him, but he wasn't there either. Later that night, I dreamed about him. In my dream, his soft lips touched my hand again, then brushed my cheek. I woke up just before his lips reached mine. So much for sleeping in—he was really getting into my head.

I'd had enough. I took out the slip of paper, debating whether to call him. My mind raced through all the possibilities: Would he be glad I called? Would he laugh and hang up? Whatever his reaction, I needed to know. Taking a deep breath, I carefully dialed the number. He picked up on the second ring.

"Hello," his deep voice echoed.

Shakily, I said, "Um hello, this is Riri. I mean Cherry. I mean, may I speak to B-Braylen."

I heard a slight chuckle on the other end of the line, and instantly, I felt I'd made a mistake—my second thought about him was right. This was all just a joke.

"Sorry, I must have dialed the wrong number," I said quickly.

"No, no, Cherry, please don't hang up. It's me. I was just laughing because I'm so glad you finally called. You definitely have the right number."

I let out a huge sigh of relief.

We instantly connected. We talked for hours that first day and soon began talking every day. We could discuss anything—school, fashion, movies, friends, goals, family, sports. Gradually, I spent less time with Summer and Aubrey and more time wrapped up in conversations with him. Naturally, they didn't know about him, though they noticed I'd become more distant. I always came up with excuses for why I couldn't hang out, and they didn't press me too much since they both had part-time jobs at the local movie theater.

Braylen and I found ways to meet up. We'd "accidentally" run into each other at the mall, grab a bite at a fast-food place, or even visit the movie theater where Summer and Aubrey worked. Eventually, though, we had to avoid the theater; Summer and Aubrey were starting to notice how often he showed up.

One day while talking to them at the concession stand, Summer said, "Y'all, I'm trying to figure out who Braylen Miller has his sights on. He hangs out here at least five or six days each month."

Aubrey said, "Yeah, girl with his fine ass. I am wondering the same thing. He never comes with anyone or leaves with anyone. I don't know what's going on with him but that sure is strange. What you think, Riri?."

I said, "Huh, oh, yeah, y'all are right. He sure is fine as hell."

We all just busted out laughing.

After that, Braylen and I decided it was best to avoid meeting up at the movies. Instead, we started going to the running trail. People there were focused solely on running, most with headphones in, so it was the perfect spot for us. We'd work out and then take long breaks on a park bench, sometimes sneaking a quick kiss or holding hands. Braylen was always a gentleman; he never asked for more than a kiss.

When summer finally arrived, we were thrilled. With both of us free, we began spending even more time together. Whenever Grandma left for work, he'd come over, and we'd spend hours laughing, watching movies, and talking.

One day, our laughing and talking went a little further. As usual, we were sitting on the sofa in the family room, watching a movie. We started kissing. The kissing got increasingly intense, and I wanted more. I climbed on top of Braylen and started to straddle him. Both of us were breathing deeply, which made me things seem intense.

I whispered in Braylen's ear, "Let's go to my bedroom."

Braylen picked me up with his strong hands and carried me up the stairs. Our kissing and rubbing and touching never stopped. Braylen started kissing my neck and nibbling on my ear. That sent a tingling sensation all over my body.

He whispered, "Do you like this feeling, Cherry?"

I moaned, "Yes, Braylen! I do!"

By the time we reached my bedroom, I felt like butter in his arms. Yet, I still wanted more. From the way I was moaning and kissing him, Braylen knew exactly what I wanted. He stopped.

I asked, "What's wrong?"

He sat me down on my bed, got on his knees, and looked in my eyes.

"You know we can't do this right?" he questioned.

"Why?"

"Cherry, I just can't. I can't take your innocence from you."

I started crying. "Why? Do you have a girlfriend or something?"

Braylen said, "Cherry, you're the only one for me. We can't do this because I know it's wrong. My parents would kill me, and your grandma would, too. I know there isn't a big age difference between us, but that does not change the fact that I am a college student, and you are a high school student. I'm an adult in the eyes of the law."

I started crying even harder. Before I knew it, the words slipped out of my mouth.

"I don't care what no one thinks. I love you."

The look in his eyes told me that he wasn't expecting me to say those words. How could he? Neither of us realized that love existed between us until that moment.

He said, "I love you, too, Riri. Will you let me do something before I leave?"

My eyes asked the question.

He answered, "No, it's not what you're thinking. I just want to taste you."

"Taste me!" I repeated. "What does that mean?"

Braylen said, "Lie down and close your eyes."

I followed his instructions.

He continued, "No matter what, Riri, I don't want you to open your eyes. Do you understand?"

I shook my head to let him know that I understood.

He continued giving instructions.

"I want you to raise your arms above your head. Let them rest on your pillows."

I obliged.

"Cherry, can I unbutton your shirt?"

I nodded.

Braylen slowly unbuttoned my shirt. I wasn't wearing a bra. He started placing light kisses on my stomach and slowly moved to my breast. I reached for him. He stopped.

"Cherry, I need you to keep your eyes closed and your hands above your head."

I obeyed.

For the first time in my short-lived life, my entire body felt alive. It was as if Braylen had awakened every inch of it. Braylen spread my legs, then slid my shorts and panties off. I felt something I had never felt before: his warm, soft lips kissing the lips of "honeypot." The touch of his lips caused a tingling sensation all over my body. He went to work with his tongue. I could feel it licking all between my thighs. I wanted to reach for him again, but I resisted because I didn't want him to stop. That tingling sensation hit me harder.

It was beginning to be too much.

He could tell because he asked, "Are you ok?"

Through heavy breaths, I answered, "I think so, but something keeps happening to me."

He said, "This is normal. You're climaxing."

This time, I couldn't resist; I opened my eyes and looked at him. He smiled, then asked, "Can I taste you again?"

I didn't know if it was the question he asked or what he did to me next, but whichever it was, that tingling sensation hit me again. It was explosive.

I don't remember anything else after that. I was startled awake by the ringing of my phone. As I opened my eyes, it took me a moment to orient myself—I was in my bed, the covers pulled up to my neck. Turning towards the window, I saw that it was still daylight. How could that be? What time was it? Then it hit me: Braylen! I smiled, but the smile quickly faded as I realized the trouble I'd be in if Grandma found him in my room—or worse, in the house.

Peeking under the covers, I expected to find myself undressed, but I had my pajamas on. I was utterly confused. Had it all been a dream? I got out of bed slowly, hearing music from downstairs, which meant Grandma was in the kitchen. But where was Braylen? Had I really imagined everything?

As I walked downstairs, I glanced at the clock: 10:38 a.m. I froze in place, and just then, Grandma walked up behind me, nearly scaring the life out of me.

She asked, "Are you feeling OK?"

Her hand immediately went to my forehead to check for signs of a fever.

I stammered, "I'm OK, Grandma. What day is it?"

She said, "Here, sit down. Today is Saturday. Yesterday, when I came home from work, you were already in bed, pj's on and all. I tried to wake you, but you only moaned, rolled over, and went back to sleep. I checked on you throughout the night, but you never felt warm or anything. You missed dinner and all, Riri. Are you sure you are feeling OK?".

"Yes, I'm fine, " I answered, "I'm just really tired."

I sat down at the kitchen table. I really hated lying to Grandma, and I was doing it more and more.

"Well, that's good to know because we need to talk," Grandma said.

The look on her face scared me. I immediately thought that she must have figured out that Braylen had been over yesterday. But then again, I wasn't even sure if he was really there.

Grandma said, "Missy, let me start by saying, we've survived too many storms to...

I cut Grandma off and finished the sentence for her, "...to be bothered by raindrops. I know, Grandma, you've told me that way too many times."

Grandma sighed heavily, then continued. As you know, summer started weeks ago. Your momma and brothers would like to come for a visit."

I jumped to my feet and screamed, "Are they out of their minds? I don't want to see them. We are doing just fine without them."

Grandma said, "I know, but it's been years since y'all have seen each other, and speaking as a mother, that is too many years for any mother to be away from her child. Missy, let's give them a chance."

I questioned, "A chance for what, Grandma? For them to ruin my life again?"

Grandma and I continued to go back and forth, but in the end, it had already been decided. She won. Momma, Greyson, and Sterling were coming in just three days.

I hurried upstairs, overwhelmed with emotions. How could they just reappear in my life like this? Sure, we spoke on the phone often, but I never intended to actually see them.

They had lied to me and turned my world upside down. Over the phone, I could pretend. But how was I supposed to keep up the act, in person, for a whole week?

I immediately called Summer.

She answered on the first ring, "Girl, what the hell is going on with you? Aubrey and I called you this morning and you didn't."

Summer stopped mid-sentence when she realized that I was crying.

"OMG, Riri, what's wrong? Is there something wrong with your grandma? Do you need us to come over?" she asked.

I couldn't even answer her; I was bawling.

Summer said, "We're on the way!"

About fifteen minutes later, the doorbell rang. I was still in bed crying.

Grandma answered the door, and I heard her say, "She's in her room."

As soon as they came into my room, they crawled into bed with me. None of us said a word. They allowed me to cry in their arms until I was ready to talk.

I said, "My momma is coming to town in three days."

"Yo momma?" Aubrey questioned.

Like I said before, I never shared the story with them about my parents. Because I arrived in Texas with Grandma so abruptly, they assumed something bad had happened to them. I don't know, maybe they thought they were dead or something. I filled them in on the secret that Momma, daddy, and my brothers had kept from me. After that, we cried together.

We must have cried ourselves to sleep, because the next thing I remember was Grandma knocking on my door.

She entered and said, "Girls, lunch is ready. The three of you should freshen up and come downstairs."

When we got downstairs, Grandma had prepared all of our favorite foods. We had a spread of homemade pizzas, salad, wings, subs, chips, cookies, and fresh lemonade. We sat down in silence.

Grandma said, "Let us pray. Father God, we come to you saying thank You. Thank You for all that You have done for us and all that You will continue to do for us. We ask that You bless our home, our neighbors, our country. We ask that You forgive us for all the wrong we have done. Allow our hearts and minds to turn to You in the time of pain and despair. God, bless Missy. Help her to forgive. Help her to heal. Help her to understand. Help her to see with new eyes. God help her to give second chances. Because God, until she is able to do these things, she will never be free. Lord, I want to thank You for Summer and Aubrey. Thank You for bringing them into our lives when we needed them most. Thank You for their friendship and sisterhood. Thank You for allowing them to be here to travel down this difficult road that we are navigating. Finally, Lord, we ask You to bless this food and allow it to be nourishment for our bodies. In Jesus's name we pray, Amen."

CHAPTER
FIVE

Prepared Me

The food Grandma prepared helped lighten the mood, giving us a chance to laugh and catch up. It felt good—actually, it felt great. For a moment, I was able to push thoughts of Momma and my brothers aside. After we finished cleaning up the kitchen, Grandma asked us to join her in the family room. The look on her face made my stomach twist into knots.

We sat with her, and I asked, "Grandma, what's wrong?"

She said, "Missy, let me start by saying we have survived too many storms to be bothered by raindrops."

I knew instantly that this could only mean one thing: bad news.

She continued, "Years ago when I brought you home with me, I was furious with Grace for keeping that terrible secret from you, well, from us. I was just as angry and hurt as you were. I especially hated what happened to you at the supermarket. I promised myself that I would protect you at all costs. But, I don't think I've done been true to my promise because I have been keeping a secret from you, too. I hope that you will forgive me and understand that I didn't want to hurt you any more than you already were. I saw the joy that Summer and Aubrey brought into your life. So, I didn't want to take that away from you."

I started crying.

"Missy, years ago your life changed, and so did the lives of everyone involved, starting with Lisa, your dad's wife. That day at the supermarket, when she looked at you and your brothers, she knew immediately who y'all were. Y'all look so much like your daddy and their daughter. So, he didn't have to explain to her who y'all were. Just like you, she felt hurt and betrayed. It destroyed her. She hated your momma but hated your daddy even more. Eventually, she and your daddy started working on their marriage. They went to couples' counseling, and eventually, your brothers joined their sessions. Liz wanted to get to know them, and she wanted them to know that she didn't hate them or blame them. All of the hate and blame was towards your momma and daddy. Your daddy knew he was wrong and accepted responsibility for his actions. More than anything, he wanted to be present for you and your brothers. Your brothers were very forgiving. All they wanted was their daddy back and, of course, their sister. I told all of them that you weren't ready. You were still too hurt and angry. You had too much healing to do. I was afraid that if they didn't give you the time you needed then they would destroy you. So, they did just that; they gave you time to heal. But the more time they gave you, the more you seemed to forget about them."

I interrupted, "So, what are you saying Grandma? Do they don't want me to be a part of their lives anymore?"

"No, Missy," Grandma answered. "That's the only thing they want. They miss you. They love you. They need you. They can't be complete without you."

"Well, they should have thought of that before they lied to me," I snapped.

"I understand, Sweetheart, but, Missy, it's time to forgive," Grandma said slowly.

"Grandma, I have forgiven them. I just don't want anything to do with them anymore."

"Well, Missy," she replied, "It's not that simple. Because, at the end of the day, they are still family. Grace is my daughter, and she is your mother. And there's nothing we can do to change that."

I interrupted, "Grandma, you can't make me like them, and you definitely can't expect me to get excited about them coming to town."

"You're so right, Riri." Grandma said. "But, can you try to give them a chance? A chance to love you? A chance for them to get to know you? A chance for them to make it right?"

Summer and Aubrey grabbed my hands. The look in their eyes said that they agreed with Grandma. I pleaded with them to take my side. Instead, they just reached over and hugged me.

I looked at Grandma and said, "Grandma, I forgive you for not telling me this years ago, and I understand why you didn't. You were right; I couldn't take any more hurt from them. I couldn't take any more secrets. If you hadn't saved me when you did, I don't know where I would be today. I hated my family, and I hated myself for loving them and trusting them."

Grandma said, "This is not your fault or your brothers' fault. The only ones to blame for that mess were your parents. But there is more to this story, Riri."

My eyes widened.

"What do you mean 'more to this story'?" I questioned.

"Well, Cherry," Grandma began. "Right after you came to live with me, emotions were high. Life was extremely hard for your momma. She missed having you in her life: seeing you everyday, talking to you, spending time with you, loving you. She got really sick, depressed even. It was bad. I thought I was going to have to go back to New York to take care of her."

Grandma took a deep breath. She was really scaring me. I had no idea what she was about to say, but, whatever it was, I could tell that it was causing her a lot of pain.

I said, "Just say it, Grandma. Things can't get much worse."

She grabbed my hands and said, "Oh Missy, I wish that were true."

I said, "Grandma, please, just tell me."

"A few months after you left New York, Grace found out that she wasn't just sick or depressed. She was pregnant! Missy, you have a six-year-old sister. Her name is Lavender."

My mouth flew open.

Grandma took a deep breath and continued, "Prepare yourself, Missy, because when your momma and brothers come to town in three days, your daddy, his wife, and both of your sisters will be coming too."

By the time I stopped crying and Summer and Aubrey left, it was late. I was exhausted and ready to get some sleep. When I got to my room, I had five missed calls from Braylen and over twenty texts. I had forgotten all about him. The day had been so emotionally draining. I called him back; he answered on the first ring.

"Riri," he started, "I'm so sorry. I won't ever do that to you again. I never meant to hurt or upset you. Please forgive me. I should've known better. Please forgive me, Cherry. I'm so sorry."

I was confused. I had to blink a few times and shake my head just to remember what he was talking about. Then it hit me. He's talking about what happened between us the previous night. It was not a dream.

I interrupted, "Braylen, Braylen, I am not upset about that. As a matter of fact, last night was unbelievable. You made me feel so good; it felt like a dream. I loved it."

"Then what's wrong? Why have you been ignoring my calls and texts?"

"I haven't been ignoring you, Braylen. I was with Grandma," I said.

"Oh, my bad; is your grandma OK? Did something happen? Do you need me…".

I interrupted before he could finish. "Braylen, Grandma is fine. But, I'm not, because my family is coming to town!"

Dr. Sartori asked softly, "Are you OK?"

At that point, I was crying. I wiped my cheeks with both hands and said, "Can you excuse me for a moment?"

I practically ran to the ladies' room. I leaned back against the door and took a deep breath. Saying all of that had been much harder than I'd anticipated. So many emotions were swirling inside me, and I hadn't even touched on the deeper secrets I'd buried. I walked over to the sink, looked at myself in the mirror, and grabbed a folded washcloth. Wetting it with cold water, I gently dabbed my face.

I looked at myself in the mirror again and told myself, "You got to get it together, Missy."

I lightly patted my face, again, placed the towel in the basket, opened the door, and walked, with confidence, back into my office.

I sat down and asked, "Can we continue?"

Dr. Sartori said, "Only if you are up to it, Dr. O'Brien. We can take this slow and stop here. As a matter of fact, I think it would be better if we continued our conversation another day."

I stood to my feet and snapped. "I am not paying you to think; I'm paying you to listen. So, do your damn job!"

She looked me in my eyes and between clenched teeth said, "Continue!"

I took my seat and continued.

CHAPTER
SIX

Loved Me

For the next three days, Braylen and I did everything we could to keep my mind off my family. We talked on the phone, went running, ate lunch together, and shared intimate moments. Braylen enjoyed making me feel good, and he made sure I knew how much he appreciated our time together. Although I wanted to reciprocate, he always stopped me. To be honest, it wasn't something I felt entirely ready for or even knew much about; I just wanted to make him feel as special as he made me feel.

He always said, "No, Riri, I just want to please you."

And boy, did he please me!

One day in particular, when Grandma was working late, as usual, Braylen and I were sitting on the couch. He began softly kissing me on my forehead. Then, each cheek. Then, my lips. Next, he moved to each ear and nibbled on them. Then, he slowly moved to my neck. He gently kissed, licked, and sucked on it, careful not to leave a trace. Next, he slipped my shirt over my head. While continuing to nibble on my neck, he reached to unsnap my bra. He put my left breast in his mouth. He took his time and worked it. He sucked, pulled, licked, and tugged at it. My nipples stood erect. Just when I thought I couldn't take it anymore, he released it. My breathing increased. I could feel my body pulsating. It felt like my "honeypot" had a heartbeat. Braylen's eyes met mine, and he kissed me deeply. Then, he inhaled my right breast. He worked my right breast the same as he had my left.

Just when I began to feel that tingling sensation all through my body, he stopped and looked me in my eyes and said, "Not yet Cherry. Lie down."

I sensed that the details of my story were too enticing to Dr. Sartori. I noticed her smiling, squirming in her seat, and crossing her legs tightly. I smiled and continued.

Braylen removed my sandals. His lips kissed each toe. He put my big toe all the way in his mouth. He sucked it and licked it like it was a Blow Pop. My eyes were closed, yet my body was awakened. His warm, wet tongue slide between each toe. By the time he got to the last one, I lost control. My body shook. He pinched my left nipple. My back arched. My "honeypot" overflowed into my panties. Braylen paused to allow my breathing to return somewhat to normal. He inched my mini skirt up a little more. I lifted my hips in the air instructing him to take my skirt up even higher. I wanted him so badly. My "honeypot" begged for his attention. Braylen spread my legs and kissed the inner parts of each thigh. I lifted my hips again expecting him to take my panties off. Instead, he moved higher to both of my breast. He rotated between the two, sucking, pulling, licking and tugging. Automatically, my body began to grind on him. I locked my legs around his body.

He whispered, "I love you, Cherry."

Those four words caused my body to erupt. It was massive! A tear rolled out of the corner of my eye.

I replied, "I love you too, Braylen. I love you so much. You're the only one I can trust, and the only one that doesn't keep secrets from me."

Braylen kissed my bottom lip, my neck, my right breast, my left breast, my stomach. Again, I raised my hips, but he skipped to my enter thighs. This was torture.

I pleaded, "Please, Braylen!"

He responded, "Only for you!"

He gave me just what I asked for. Instead of taking off my panties, like he had always done before, he simply slid them over. He started to use his tongue to lick up all of my sweetness. He licked and sucked it all, but my "honeypot" continued to make more goodness. My panties rubbed against my clit. It felt so sensual. I begged Braylen to give me more. The more I begged, the harder he kissed, licked, sucked, and rubbed my clit. I grabbed each of his ears with each of my hands. I guided his head exactly where I wanted his tongue. I erupted. All the hate, disappointment, mistrust, and pain I had for my family abandoned my body. I felt free, relaxed, and tired.

Dr. Sartori interrupted. "Excuse me, Dr. O'Brien."

She headed straight for the ladies' room. I knew exactly what she needed to do! I made myself a cup of coffee and stared out the window. When she returned, I purposely gave her an accusatory look.

She looked away, cleared her throat, and asked, "Dr. O'Brien, are you saying that he never penetrated you?"

"Never!" I answered quickly. "I experienced many sexual encounters with Braylen when I was sixteen. As many times as I asked him to, begged him to, cried for him to, he would never penetrate me or let me suck his penis. He told me that I was different from other girls. He respected me and pleasing me was enough for him."

CHAPTER
SEVEN

Licked Me

The dreaded day was approaching, and I tried not to dwell on my family and the pain they brought. Instead, I focused on Braylen and how good he made me feel. Thinking of him was the only way I could push them from my mind. Grandma spent days preparing—grocery shopping, cleaning the house, putting fresh linens on the beds, and cooking. I, on the other hand, didn't lift a finger to help, and I don't think Grandma expected me to. She let me sulk in my own misery.

On the day they were set to arrive, Grandma dressed in her Sunday's best, while I wore a simple T-shirt, sweats, and slides. She insisted that I wait downstairs with her for their arrival, even though I would have preferred hiding away in my room. Grandma wasn't having it.

"Missy," she stated, "They are coming, and we are going to make the most of it. Besides, no one can ever take the place of your mother."

I interrupted, "Well, you certainly did."

She continued, "Well, that was not my intention, and it definitely wasn't my intention to make my home your permanent home. My intention was to allow you to heal from the hurt, help you forgive, and send you back to your momma who needs and misses you."

I looked at Grandma with tears in my eyes and asked, "Are you saying that I…"

I was not able to finish my question because we heard the sound of car doors closing. Grandma ran to the front door. She motioned for me to follow.

I don't think I'd ever seen Grandma so happy. She opened the door and quickly ran down the steps. I followed her outside but stayed on the porch. Grandma rushed over to Momma, and they hugged tightly, over and over. Greyson and Sterling stepped out of the car, followed by a little girl. Daddy got out of another car, looking just the same, and opened the doors for a woman and a girl who appeared to be my age. Grandma greeted each of them with the same warmth she'd shown Momma. From the outside, everyone seemed so happy, but I felt completely out of place. My mind was full of questions. What should I say to them? What was I supposed to do? I felt like a complete mess, and just thinking about it made everything spin.

Spin

Spin

Spin

Spin

Spin!

I felt sick to my stomach. I ran into the house. I heard Grandma call my name. As fast as my feet would carry me, I raced to the upstairs bathroom. I closed the door and locked it. I made it to the toilet just in time. Everything that I had eaten that day and the day before came up. I felt terrible. Grandma lightly knocked on the door.

She said, "Missy, are you OK? I know this is hard, but you are built for moments like these. You have survived too may storms to be bothered by raindrops. You got this, and no one is expecting anything from you."

Grandma's voice was cracking. That scared me. It sounded like she was crying. I had never heard her cry before. I quickly opened the door, and sure enough, Grandma was crying. We embraced each other.

After our moment, we dried our faces.

Grandma said, "Let's go downstairs. You have nothing to worry about. Everyone is just as nervous as you are. Believe me, this is not easy for any of them. It's probably harder for them than it is for you. Come on, we got this."

Grandma and I reached the stair. Everyone rose to greet us. As soon as my foot hit the last step, Momma ran over and hugged me tightly. I did not know what to do, so I just stood there. The hug seemed to last forever. She was crying.

She said through sobs, "Missy, I have missed you so much. You're beautiful. I can't believe this day has finally arrived. It's been so long, too long. I have missed you so much, Missy. All the times we have talked on the phone could have never prepared me for this moment. I'm so happy to see you. Oh, how I've missed you."

Without thinking, I hugged her back. Greyson, Sterling and the little girl joined u. For the moment, it felt good to be back with them. To see them. I never realized how much I had missed them. Hugging them. Seeing them. Loving them. We hugged until Grandma finally said, "Let's have a seat. We have so much catching up to do."

The five of us squeezed together on the sofa. Things felt OK. It was Greyson, Sterling, me, Momma, and the little girl sat on Greyson's lap. Greyson began twisting his fingers together. "Some things never change," I said to myself.

I totally forgot that Daddy's family was even in the room.

Grandma spoke again, "William, you, Lisa and Olivia are welcome to sit here."

"His secret family. Wait, or were we the secret?" I thought to myself.

The memory of me learning about Daddy's other family tried to sneak back into my mind, but I quickly shook my head to erase it.

Daddy, cleared his throat, "Riri," he said, "this is my wife, Lisa, and our daughter, your sister, Olivia." Daddy walked over, knelt down, and hugged me. Instantly, his smell brought back so many good memories. I realized how much I had missed Daddy. The tears started, again.

Again, Grandma interjected, "Why don't we all take a seat and give Cherry an opportunity to take this all in. I know this has to be a bit overwhelming for her right now."

"Grandma always knows the right things to say," I thought to myself.

Everyone was seated and chatting, giving me a moment to take it all in, just as Grandma had suggested. They had all changed—but what else could I expect? It had been six years since I'd last seen them. Now, Greyson and Sterling looked just like a younger version of Daddy. Greyson was twenty-one, and Sterling was twenty. Momma and Daddy hadn't changed much; they were as attractive as ever. The little girl sitting on Greyson's lap looked like a younger version of me. Daddy's wife was beautiful too, with a strong resemblance to Momma. I could see why he'd been drawn to both of them. The other girl, Olivia, also looked a lot like me. It's incredible, the way genetics work.

Even though everyone was chatting about small matters, the tension in the room was still thick. Finally, Momma cut it.

She said, "Missy,"

Hearing her call me that in person felt different than hearing it over the phone.

"I want to start off by saying sorry. We have all said it many times before, but it's what we still feel today. Your daddy and I are sorry for all of the hurt we have caused everyone in this room. We want to start over today. We want to be a happy family again under the same roof."

I jumped to my feet. Grandma tried to pull me back down.

"Are you saying you want me to come live with you?" I asked in a matter-of-fact tone.

Before Momma could answer, Grandma quickly responded, "We have plenty of time to get into those things. Let's just enjoy the moment we have before us."

I did not like the words that came out of Grandma's mouth. Something told me that they were keeping another secret.

Finally, the little girl jumped off Grey's lap. She reached for Momma, buried her face in Momma's chest and started crying. It was like everyone had forgotten she was in the room.

Momma said, "It's OK Lavender. Let's meet your sister, Cherry, and your grandma."

Momma inched Lavender away from her so she could look at me.

She continued, "Cherry and Lavender this introduction is long overdue. Cherry, this is your sister, Lavender. Lavender, this is your other big sister, Cherry."

Lavender looked at me, and I looked at her. She did something I didn't expect. She reached over and hugged me.

She said in the most angelic voice, "I am so happy to finally meet you. Momma and Daddy and Grey and Ster talk about you all the time. Me and Liv have been talking about meeting you ever since Mommy and Daddy told us we were coming here. You look just like Liv. Don't she, Liv?"

She looked over at Olivia waiting for her response. Everything started spinning again!

Spin

Spin

Spin

Spin

Spin

Spin

Spin

Spin

I think Momma could tell that I was about to be sick, again, because she yanked Lavender from in front of me. I ran back upstairs, making it just in time, again. This time, I did not hear Grandma's footsteps running behind me. Instead, it was the tiny footsteps of Lavender.

THE NEXT FEW DAYS WENT BY QUICKLY. I SPENT A LOT OF TIME with my family and got to know Daddy's wife better. She turned out to be pretty cool and genuinely kind. She explained that she'd never intended to hurt me and that she hadn't known about us. She'd had some suspicions that something was going on with Daddy, but she never imagined he was hiding an entire family. I also learned that Olivia and I were only six months apart—Daddy had been quite the "rolling stone," if you catch my drift.

Liv was nice, too. We seemed to have a lot in common. She met Summer and Aubrey; they liked her. However, they were more interested in my "fine ass brothers."

Greyson and Sterling were as protective as ever, and even more so when it came to Lavender and Olivia. Every night, the five of us would stay up in my room, talking until the early hours. During the day, they followed me around everywhere— shopping, movies, lunch at my favorite spots, and even joining me on my daily runs. This meant I couldn't spend any time with Braylen. While I loved being with them, I missed Braylen. We hardly spoke on the phone, and I texted only a little since they'd always ask who I was texting.

After a week of this, I needed to see Braylen. I missed him and wanted to share everything about my family's visit. On Saturday morning, I told everyone I'd made plans to hang out with Summer and Aubrey later that evening. I spent the day with my family, enjoying the laughter, food, and games.

Around seven, I told them I was heading to Aubrey's and would be back by curfew. Momma initially suggested I take Liv and Lavender, but Liv declined, understanding that

I needed some girl time. Lavender, however, begged to come along, even breaking into tears. I was about to call Braylen to cancel when Liv suggested that they could paint each other's nails, giving me a grateful escape. I felt a bit guilty for lying, knowing we were all trying to mend things. After a round of hugs, I slipped out the door, excited to finally see Braylen.

Greyson and Sterling followed me to the door, offering to walk me to Aubrey's house. I convinced them I'd be fine, as it was just a few houses away, and they finally relented. My heart pounded as I neared the end of the street, spotting Braylen's SUV parked exactly as we'd planned. I ran over and jumped in, and we shared passionate kisses, thrilled to finally be together.

I spent the next hour talking nonstop, sharing every detail of my family's visit. Braylen's warm smile showed he was happy just to listen. He told me I seemed truly happy to have my family back, and I agreed. Then, we kissed again. Our kisses grew more intense, and in that moment, we were completely lost in each other.

Braylen said, "Oh, Cherry, I've missed you so much."

His words did something to me.

"I've missed you, too, Braylen."

He started rubbing my thighs. My breathing increased. I wanted so much more from Braylen, but I knew we were not in a place to make that happen. Braylen's hand went further up my thigh. I licked his earlobe. He moaned. I moaned in return. He spread my legs and rubbed my clit through my panties, our new favorite thing. The friction was too much.

He said, "Riri, we need to stop."

I said, "I know."

Our passion for each other increased. I am not sure how it happened, but we ended up on the third row of his SUV. I was lying on the seat as if it were my bed.

Braylen said the words I longed for, "Riri, can I lick you?"

Without hesitation, I raised my hips in the air, slid my panties down, spread my legs, and said, "Lick me!"

When his lips touched the lips of my "honeypot", I lost control. Just his touch made my body shake. He looked me in my eyes and said, "Riri, I'm not done with you yet, Baby. I'm starving tonight."

But before he could satisfy his hunger, the unthinkable happened. My brothers screamed my name.

Greyson asked, "What the fuck is going on? What are you doing to my sister?"

Sterling yelled, "Open this damn door!"

Braylen and I jumped up. The look on our faces was pure fear.

I stammered, "Braylen, it's my brothers!"

Braylen climbed over the seats. He jumped into the driver's seat and started his SUV.

I said, "What are you doing?"

He said, "Cherry, we have to get out of here."

I said, "Are you insane? I can't leave. Let me get out to talk to them."

Braylen said, "Your brothers aren't in talking mode, Cherry."

I said, "They aren't going to hurt me."

He said, "Cherry, it's not you that they want to hurt."

All the while, Greyson and Sterling were cursing and banging on his doors and windows.

I assured Braylen that I could handle Grey and Sterl; boy oh boy, was I wrong.

I quickly pulled my skirt down, not even bothering to find my underwear, which were in the truck somewhere. Climbing to the second row of seats, I took a deep breath and opened the door. The expressions on their faces terrified me—they were beyond furious. Before I could step out, Greyson lifted me down onto the asphalt and then climbed in. Sterling was waiting at the driver's door, and as soon as Greyson leapt over the seat, he began landing punches on Braylen, giving him no chance to respond. While he did, he unlocked the driver's side door, allowing Sterling to reach in and pull Braylen out of the truck. I hurried to the other side, watching as my brothers continued to lay into him.

Sterling said, "Have you lost your fucking mind? What the fuck are you doing? Who are you?"

I begged them to stop, but they wouldn't listen. They were kicking and punching. Braylen was getting his ass beat, and there was nothing I could do to help. Suddenly, Sterling stopped. I think it was because he was tired. He pulled Greyson off of Braylen. I fell to Braylen's side. He was a bloody mess.

I said, "I'm sorry, Braylen. I'm so sorry."

Greyson reached inside the SUV and grabbed Braylen's wallet. He opened it and pulled out his driver's license.

He read, "Braylen Miller."

Then he said, "Are you fucking kidding me? Dude, you are nineteen years old. My sister is only sixteen."

Greyson and Sterling pushed me aside and started beating his ass again. The second time around was so much worse than the first. They cursed him, kicked him, and punched him repeatedly. I begged them to stop. I was crying and yelling, hysterically. After what felt like forever, a neighbor must have heard the commotion and turned on his porch light.

He yelled, "What's going on out there?"

Finally, they stopped. Braylen was coughing up blood. Before the beating could start again, he dragged himself into his truck. I heard the doors lock. He sped off. I was hysterical.

The neighbor yelled out, "Is everything OK? Is someone hurt? Do you need me to call the cops?"

Breathing heavily, Sterling said, "No, sir. We have everything under control, sir."

They fell on the ground next to me and cried. We all cried. I cried because of Braylen. It was all my fault. They cried because of me. It was all their fault because they weren't there to protect me.

Finally, I got up and started walking home. They followed.

Sterling said, "Wait, Riri. We need to talk." I continued walking.

He said, "Cherry, I said wait. This is not over."

I turned toward them and shouted through sobs, "What do you mean it's not over? Are you going to beat him some more? Are you going to tell Grandma, Mommy, and Daddy? How can this not be over? What else are you going to do?"

They both looked at each other.

Greyson spoke next, "Missy, you can't think for one minute that this is our fault? Who was that guy?"

I yelled, "My boyfriend!"

Greyson said, "Little girl, you don't have a boyfriend. That bastard is nineteen. Do you think that what y'all was doing was OK?"

I said, "Who are you to tell me what's OK? You're not my daddy!"

Sterling interrupted, "Missy, we don't have to be your daddy to know what y'all were doing is not OK."

I screamed, "Why do y'all keep ruining my life? Why do you think it is your job to watch after me? Better yet, were y'all following me?"

I started crying harder. They both rushed over to me and hugged me.

I screamed, "Get off of me!"

I tried to break free. But they wouldn't let go, and I didn't have the strength to fight.

Greyson said, "First of all, Missy, we've never tried to be your daddy. But it is our job to look after you and to protect you. Second, we have regretted keeping secrets from you and ruining your life. Third, we were not following you. We were going for a jog, and we heard your voice coming from the car. Do you know how scared we were when we thought someone was hurting you? And how angry we became when we saw what he was doing. That's some shit I'll never be able to erase from my mind."

I said, "But, he wasn't hurting me. You don't know anything about him. He is—"

Sterling interrupted, "We don't have to know anything about him to know that he had no business doing what he was doing. Do you know what could have happened if the police would have found y'all instead of us? Missy, you are a minor, and he's nineteen."

I asked, "So, are you going to call the police?"

They looked at each other.

"Are you? Cause I wanted him to do that to me. He didn't force me."

Greyson yelled through clenched teeth, "Stop saying that because that doesn't make it right, damn it."

Sterling touched Greyson's arm to calm him and said, "Look, Cherry, the right thing for us to do is to go home, explain to our parents what just happened, and then call the police."

I started hyperventilating.

He continued, "But, we won't!"

Grey interrupted, "What you mean we wo—"

Sterling looked at him and continued, "Like I said, we won't. As hard as it may be, we won't tell our parents what just happened. But we will have a conversation with Braylen Miller. And I am sure he isn't going to like what we have to say."

I tried walking away. Sterling grabbed me a little harder than I expected.

He said, "Hold up, Cherry! You don't get the opportunity to walk away from us this easily. This is not our fault, and you aren't completely innocent either. So, you will listen to what we have to say whether you like it or not."

I had never heard my brother talk to me in that tone. Both of them had a look of disgust on their faces.

Sterling continued, "We're going home. We will try to pretend like this didn't happen. Even though I will have a hard time doing that. We will say we ran into you on our way back from our jog and that you're upset because you had an argument with your friends. We will assure everyone that you are fine and that you need a minute to yourself. Then, tomorrow, Miss Cherry, we will pay Braylen Miller a visit."

Greyson looked at Braylen's driver's license again. He still had it. That meant he knew exactly where to find him.

When we got back to the house, I opened the door and ran upstairs to my room. Grandma, Momma, and Daddy called after me, I didn't answer. My brother explained the lie that Sterling conjured up. No one bothered me the remainder of the night, except for Liv. She came into my room to see if I was OK. She knocked softly and opened the door.

"Cherry," she said, "are you OK?"

I said through sobs, "Just leave me alone. I don't want to talk. My life is over."

She said, "Well, if you want to talk about what happened with your friends, I'm here for you."

"I said I don't want to talk. Every time y'all come around, things get bad. Now, just leave me alone."

Confused, Liv said, "Huh? What are you talking about?"

I didn't respond.

She continued, "Anyway; like I said, if you want to talk, I'm here for you."

She closed the door. I felt really bad about the way I had talked to her. None of this was her fault. Why did I have to be so mean to her? I thought about calling her back to apologize, but I assured myself that it could wait until morning. I had bigger problems. Braylen was not answering my calls. In fact, his phone was going straight to voicemail. Where was he? Did my brothers hurt him too badly? Omg, was he dead? I spent the remainder of the night worried sick about him.

Morning came slowly. I don't think I slept at all; I was frantic. I just wanted to talk to Braylen. There was a knock at my door; I rolled my eyes thinking it was Sterling and Greyson. It was Momma.

She stuck her head inside and asked, "Do you want to talk about it, sweetheart?"

I said, "No. No one understands. No one knows the kind of person he is. He listens to me. He didn't do anything that I did not want him to do."

"Whoooaaa!" Momma said, "What are you talking about, and who is he?"

I had forgotten about Sterling's lie. Momma looked straight into my eyes. That look told me she wanted answers and wanted them quickly. I sat up in bed.

Looking away, I said, "Like Greyson and Sterling said, Momma, I had a disagreement with friends. But it is OK. I will get everything straightened out."

Momma said, "Missy, it seems like there's more to this story. Tell me exactly what's going on now!"

"There's this boy that Aubrey has a crush on. Turns out, he like me instead. So, last night on my way to Aubrey's house, I ran into him. He and I were talking. He gave me a kiss on the cheek. Aubrey happened to be looking out of her window when it happened. She saw the kiss, and now, she's mad at me. She thinks I betrayed her. She says I was flirting with him. I tried to explain, but she wasn't trying to hear any of it. Worst part, Summer is taking her side. Now both of them are mad at me."

I couldn't believe how easy it was for me to come up with that lie. Maybe I'm more like Mommy and Daddy, after all.

Momma said, "Aww, sweetie, I understand. You girls are pretty close. I promise they won't stay mad at you long. Just give them some time; they will come around. But Missy, there is something else I want to talk to you about."

I looked at Momma worriedly. Maybe she knew about Braylen after all.

She continued, "I know it had to be a complete shock to you to find out about Lavender."

I breathed a sigh of relief. It wasn't about Braylen.

"I just didn't know how to tell you about her. It seemed like every time I planned to, it was the wrong time. You would sound super happy on the phone, and I didn't want to ruin that moment. Or, I would hear that familiar sound of sadness, and I didn't want to make it worse. I wanted to tell you about her from the moment I laid eyes on her, but I just couldn't bring myself to tell you. Moments turned to days. Days turned to weeks. Weeks turned to months. Months turned to years. Your brother begged me to tell you. Momma begged me to tell you. I even begged myself to tell you, as silly as that sounds. Lavender has been dying to meet you. She's heard so many great stories about her big sister. I'm so glad the two of you have finally met."

I interrupted her. "So, all of this time Lavender has known about me, but I have not known about her? Do you know how that makes me feel? Do you know the kind of monster she probably thinks I am?"

Momma tried to interrupt me, but I wouldn't let her.

"A terrible monster, Momma! What kind of big sister have I been to her? No kind. I wasn't given a chance to be. I don't know her, and she don't know me. It's all because of you and your lies. You have stolen years from us that we can never get back! Do you realize that? You have destroyed a piece of both of us that can never be repaired; a bond that can't be fixed."

With that, I got up from my bed, walked out of my room, and slammed the door!

I managed to make it downstairs to breakfast. Everyone was sitting around the kitchen eating and talking. They were leaving the next day, and it couldn't come fast enough. As self-ish as it may sound, I was ready to get back to just Grandma and me. After breakfast, I continued calling Braylen. His calls were still going straight to voicemail. I was worried; I felt myself getting physically sick. I couldn't keep my breakfast down. My head was in the toilet barfing up what remained of breakfast when I heard Greyson and Sterling knocking on the bathroom door.

"Missy," Sterling said, "are you OK?" Open the door. We need to talk to you."

I opened the door because I did not feel like fighting with them anymore. They entered the bathroom and locked the door. That made me feel worse. I rinsed my mouth out with water to remove the remains of the vomit.

I looked at them. "What's wrong? Did something happen to Braylen?"

When I said his name, a look of total disgust crossed their faces.

"Please tell me," I begged.

While twisting his fingers, Greyson spoke next. "Cherry, you need to tell us everything that has happened between you and Braylen. It's very clear to us what y'all were doing last night and what was probably coming next. We are disgusted with what we saw and heard. Now, since we've heard you in hearing vomiting, we are concerned. What else have y'all been doing, and how many times has it happened?"

"How many times has what happened?" I asked.

Sterling blurted out, "Sex, Cherry! Did y'all have sex or not, and if so, did you use protection?"

"No," I screamed, "we didn't have sex. Are y'all crazy? Is Braylen OK?"

They looked at me with confused faces.

"Cherry," Greyson said, "why in the hell would we care if Braylen is OK? He's a damn molester. You have to know that what Braylen did to you was wrong on so many levels. You shouldn't be thinking about him at a time like this. You're the victim here."

"I'm not a victim," I interrupted, "and he's not a molester. He didn't hurt me. He loves me, and I love him."

Both of them lowered and shook their heads. I guess they couldn't believe the words that were coming out of my mouth.

Sterling said, "Look, Riri, we are about to head over to his address; so, let's go. Braylen Miller has a lot to explain, or he will get his ass beat again!"

Greyson opened the bathroom door, and they walked out. I could not believe what was about to happen. I could not let them go over to Dr. Miller's house; there was no telling what would happen if they did that. When I stepped out of the bathroom, the familiar sound of chatter and laughter coming from the family room did not exist. When I went down the stairs to try to stop my brothers, the family room was empty.

I asked, "Where's everybody?"

My brothers continued walking out of the front door, while Sterling answered, "They are out for a while. Let's go!

I followed them to the car.

I said, "Wait, y'all can't do this!"

Greyson said, "You have two options, Riri. Either get in the car or stay here, but either way we are going to pay Braylen a visit."

By his tone, I knew there was no need to argue. I got in the back seat of the car and closed the door.

CHAPTER
EIGHT

Molested Me

The drive to the Millers' house felt endless. No one said a word, and my heart was pounding in my ears. The silence gave me time to think. Were my brothers right? Was what Braylen and I had been doing wrong? Could a guy like him really be interested in a girl like me? The more I thought about it, the worse I felt. How could I have been so naive? Braylen had everything, including access to any college girl he wanted. How could I have let him use me, believing every word he said—especially "I love you"? I'd told so many lies just to spend time alone with him. My eyes filled with tears, and I began to cry harder.

Greyson pulled over, and both my brothers got out and joined me in the backseat. They didn't say a word; they just sat with me, letting me cry, giving me space to release all the hurt and disappointment I felt inside.

I whispered between sobs, "I'm so sorry. I don't know what I was thinking."

They started crying, too— for the innocence that had been taken away from me and for not being around to protect me and watch me grow up. After about 10 minutes, they got back into the front. Although I was hoping that we would just head back home, I know that wasn't going to happen. It was time for me to face the inevitable. I just hoped Braylen was ready to face my brothers.

When we pulled into the Miller's driveway, I was in awe. Their home was surrounded by a black iron fence. The grass was well-manicured. The house was two stories high with large windows and detailed stonework. Braylen's SUV was parked in the driveway, which meant he had made it home last night. We got out of the car and headed to the door. I hid behind my brothers. Sterling rang the doorbell. Dr. Miller opened the door as if he were expecting someone.

He said, "May I help you?"

Sterling said, "Yeah, we are here to see Braylen Miller."

Dr. Miller said, "Well, he is not available at the moment. I will let him know that you stopped by. You are?"

Greyson stepped in front of Sterling.

He said, "Sir, this is an urgent matter. In fact, it's a matter of life or death. We need to speak to Braylen now, and we won't leave until we do."

Dr. Miller spoke in a matter-of-fact tone.

"Excuse me, I don't know who you think you are, but you don't come to my home making demands. Now, like I've already said, Braylen is not available at this time. If you want to tell me what this is about, then maybe I can assist you. If not, get the hell off my property."

Neither of my brothers spoke. They simply stepped to the side. When Dr. Miller saw me standing there, his mouth dropped.

He questioned, "Cherry, are you OK? What are you doing here? Why are you crying? What's going on here? Are you hurt? Who are these guys?"

I said between sobs, "I'm fine, Dr. Miller. These are my brothers. Can we come in and talk to you?"

Dr. Miller stepped aside to let us into his home and led us to the family room. I could tell it was the family room from the many family photos lining the walls. A large television stood against one wall, and a shelf displayed various trophies and awards. I sat down on the sofa while my brothers and Dr. Miller remained standing.

He spoke, "Would someone please tell me what is going on here? Cherry, are you OK?"

Greyson placed his hand on my shoulder to keep me silent. Dr. Miller noticed.

Greyson said, "Sir, we apologize for barging in on you unexpectedly, but it's very important that we speak to Braylen, now!"

I jumped at the boom in my brother's voice. The anger in him was rising again.

Dr. Miller matched his tone. "Like I told you at the door, Braylen is not available at this time. Could someone please tell me what this is about, or I'm calling the police!"

This time, Sterling spoke.

"How bout you get your punk ass son out here so he can explain to us why he's been molesting our little sister, or you can just call the police like you suggested!"

THE MEMORIES OF THAT DAY BEGAN TO OVERTAKE ME. DR. SARtori reached me a Kleenex.

"I'm sorry," I said.

Dr. Sartori replied, "Take your time, Dr. O'Brien. Molestation can be a very painful subject to talk about and relive."

I hated that word. I didn't like having to explain to anyone else that what Braylen did to me was not molestation. Yes, I was a minor, but he was only a few years older than me. I wanted him to do it. I enjoyed it. Even years later, my mind still hadn't changed. To me, molestation was when a much older person did inappropriate things to a younger person. Braylen and I were too close in age for me to consider it molestation. On top of that, he always asked for permission, and I gave it to him.

Nevertheless, I needed a break, so I went to the ladies' room. When I returned, I was ready to continue.

"MOLESTING YOUR SISTER?" DR. MILLER QUESTIONED.

He sank into the chair beside him. He looked like he was about to faint. His breathing increased.

"Yeah," Sterling replied, "we are here to have a long talk with Braylen. So, like my brother just said, why don't you get his ass in here now, or you both will be sorry."

Dr. Miller slid to the edge of his seat and said, "Look, young man, I don't know you and you certainly don't know me, but one thing for sure, you don't come into my home threatening me. What do you mean Braylen has been molesting your sister? That doesn't sound like anything my son would do. Cherry, what are they talking about?"

Too afraid to speak, I dropped my head into my hands.

Greyson looked at Sterling and me, then said, "I'm 'bout to lose it!"

Dr. Miller said, "None of this is making sense to me. Excuse me for a moment."

When he left the room, Greyson started twisting his fingers and pacing back and forth.

Sterling looked at him and said, "Man, you got to chill with the pacing. You making me anxious."

Greyson continued to pace.

A few moments later, Dr. Miller and his wife, Cindy, and Braylen entered the room. Braylen was barely walking on his own; they were practically carrying him. His face was a maze of blue, black, and red. His eyes were completely swollen shut. There was dried blood around his eyes, nose, and mouth. His left arm and ribs were bandaged.

I cried out, "Oh my God, Braylen, I am so sorry. Are you OK?"

Greyson balled his fists. Sterling grabbed his shoulders to stop him from attacking Braylen, again. I could tell that Dr. Miller and Cindy were shocked as to why I cried out to Braylen with such familiarity. They helped Braylen take a seat. He grunted because of pain. Although his eyes were shut, he dared not look in our direction.

"Now," Mrs. Miller began, "Can someone please tell us what's going on? When our son came home last night, it was pretty clear that he had been attacked. We couldn't get anything out of him. We asked several times who did this to him, but he wouldn't tell us. Are the three of you responsible for this? I'm calling the police."

Mrs. Miller picked up the phone from the end table.

Sterling shouted, "Don't you dare blame my sister for what this pervert did. Your son is the one responsible for what happened to him. Yeah, call the police; my brother and I think that is a great idea. Trust me, we have wanted to from the moment we saw what he was doing to our sister."

Mrs. Miller was speechless. Her mouth fell open.

Braylen said in an excruciating tone, "Mom, please put the phone down. We don't need the police. I can explain."

And he did just that. I didn't have to say a word. Braylen confessed everything to his parents—our phone calls, evening meet-ups, and everything we'd shared together. By the time he finished, everyone in the room was in tears. Braylen was crying from the pain he'd caused his parents. The Millers were crying out of shame, hurt, disappointment, and guilt. My brothers were crying, overwhelmed with anger as they listened. I was crying because I truly loved Braylen Miller, and I knew that what we had was now over.

I looked at Dr. Sartori. She looked at me. Both of us were expecting the other to say something. She spoke first.

She said, "Do you want my advice on what happened to you or—"

I interjected, "No advice needed, Dr. Sartori. This is just the beginning of how things began to unfold in my life."

I explained to Dr. Sartori that the Millers apologized to my brothers and me so many times that day. They promised that they would fix things. They begged my brothers not to involve the authorities. Reluctantly, my brothers agreed. They explained to my brothers that they would be in touch with them soon. Then, we said our goodbyes and drove home in silence.

The next day, my family left. I think Momma had considered asking me to return to New York, but my brothers must have talked her out of it. They knew I'd already been through enough during their visit. While they initially went back to New York with the rest of the family, Greyson and Sterling permanently returned to Texas two weeks later. I wasn't thrilled about it, but Grandma was overjoyed. They convinced everyone that being close to Grandma and me would be better for all of us and that they loved being here. However, with Momma, Lavender, Olivia, Daddy, and Lisa in New York, it left Momma feeling sad.

I tried calling Braylen for weeks, but he never answered. It was as if he'd vanished. I felt foolish and became withdrawn, sad, and deeply depressed. Everyone noticed—Grandma, Summer, Aubrey, Greyson, and Sterling. Grandma assumed it was because I missed the family back in New York. Summer and Aubrey begged me to open up, but I refused. Greyson and Sterling understood what was going on; they tried to get me to talk and even suggested professional help, but I shut down the idea. At school, Dr. Miller avoided me entirely, unable to even meet my gaze. If we crossed paths, he'd quickly turn away, and he stopped coming to my after-school practices and club meetings.

I turned seventeen that summer and didn't even want a birthday party, which concerned Grandma since we'd always celebrated my birthdays in a big way. Weeks afterwards, Dr. Miller and his wife eventually began calling to check on me, but I barely had anything to say. Whenever I asked about Braylen, they would dodge the question, so I eventually stopped answering their calls.

As summer break wound down, I found no interest in back-to-school shopping, senior year plans, or any of the things most rising seniors looked forward to. My mind stayed fixed on Braylen, and with each thought, my anger grew. I hated him for abandoning me, but I hated myself more for letting him use me. I made a vow: I would never let anyone use me again. I raised my guard high and had no intention of letting it down. From then on, instead of being used, I decided I would be the one in control—and I started with the Millers.

CHAPTER
NINE

Paid Me

Once school started back, it was clear that Dr. Miller blamed himself for what happened. He called me to his office.

"Cherry," he said with a cracking voice, "you have no idea how sorry I am for what my son did to you. This is all my fault. I shouldn't have allowed Braylen to hang around school so much."

I interrupted him.

"Dr. Miller, Where's Braylen? I've been calling him."

He interrupted me.

"Cherry, don't worry about Braylen. My wife and I have taken care of the situation."

"Taken care of the situation?!" I practically screamed. "Please tell me where Braylen is. I need to speak to him. I need to apologize to him for what my brothers did."

I was crying hysterically.

Dr Miller said, "Cherry, you have absolutely nothing to apologize for. This is all my fault. I take full responsibility for everything that has happened. Braylen had no business hanging around school. I'm assuming that is how y'all met. I allowed my personal life to get in the way of my professional one. I'm willing to do anything I can to fix this. So, if there is anything you need, please don't hesitate to ask me, Cherry. I'll make this right with you if it takes the rest of my life. Please, forgive me. I'm so sorry."

Although his apology was sincere, I didn't let it phase me. I was furious with him for not telling me where Braylen was, and I was planning to make him pay. My face hid what I was really feeling. It showed pain, innocence, betrayal, and confusion. Inside, I wanted revenge, and I had him exactly where I wanted him.

Sitting in my office now, I couldn't help but let a little smile peek through. Dr. Satori noticed it!

To put it briefly, I took full advantage of Dr. Miller's guilt. Anytime I needed money—or even when I didn't—he'd give it to me. I won student body president, homecoming queen, and anything else I set my sights on. Don't get me wrong, I made good grades, and my classmates liked me, but Dr. Miller went above and beyond when it came to supporting me at school. He constantly praised me to the faculty and student body and showered me with gifts during the holidays. If I could've come up with a way to explain it to Grandma and my brothers, I probably could've even gotten a car.

The Millers bought me the latest clothes, shoes, purses, and phones, and they covered my hair and nail appointments too. I told Grandma that Momma and my brothers were buying me these things, and I told my brothers that Grandma and Momma were responsible. I earned multiple college scholarships and became the first female recipient of the scholarship from Dr. Miller's fraternity, which had always gone to a male student. When they announced my name, everyone was stunned.

I was accepted to every college and university I applied to, thanks in part to Dr. Miller's glowing recommendations and influence with the board. By the time I left for college, I imagine he felt some relief. He no longer had to see his Achilles heel roaming the school's hallways. Finally, he was free from the weight I had placed on his shoulders.

When it came time to make my final college decision, Dr. Miller arranged visits to each campus. I enjoyed them all and was truly impressed with what each school had to offer. After those visits, I knew I wanted to attend an HBCU so I could be surrounded by people who shared similar backgrounds and cultural experiences. In the end, I chose Spelman College in Atlanta, Georgia, a historically Black women's college vowing I was done with boys for good—or so I thought.

CHAPTER
TEN

Refused Me

My freshman and sophomore years at Spelman were fairly typical. I was a dual-engineering major, so studying and maintaining my GPA were top priorities. Campus life was fantastic, and I became well known. I served as class president for both freshman and sophomore years and was also a cheerleader. In my sophomore year, I joined a sorority, which I loved. Spending time with my sorority sisters was a highlight.

Oh, and I should mention that Summer and Aubrey also attended Spelman. We got an apartment together. Also, we pledged together, which brought us even closer than before. We attended every Greek event together, and Greek life made college even more exciting. Meanwhile, Dr. Miller, still feeling guilty about Braylen's actions, continued to send me money and gifts. Every month, I received all sorts of items—sorority paraphernalia, clothes, shoes, purses, and anything else I wanted.

Junior year brought some unexpected twists. There's something about that third year —it's like everything changed. I met Dr. Nelson, an engineering professor with whom I'd already taken several classes, so we knew each other fairly well. Back in my sophomore year, I sometimes thought he was eyeing me, but, much like my initial experience with Braylen, I brushed it off.

As a junior, my classes became much more challenging, and I joined study groups with my peers, but I still struggled to grasp some of the material. To keep up, I began meeting with Dr. Nelson for extra help. During one of our sessions, he seemed unusually restless, fidgeting constantly, and appearing distracted—or maybe even annoyed. I wasn't quite sure.

We would always meet in an available classroom. At the conclusion of our session, he said, "Miss. O'Brien, unfortunately, this will have to be our last session together."

Then, he looked down and started writing something.

My mouth dropped. I think he was expecting me to just leave, but I didn't. I was frozen.

He got up from his chair and said, "Please excuse me. When you are done here, please see your way out."

After that, he just left. I was dumbfounded.

"What just happened?" I thought to myself.

I probably sat there for about five more minutes. It took that long for my brain to connect back to the rest of my body. I did not attend his class the following week. I was too embarrassed. I could not understand why he would say something like that to me.

A few days later, on a Friday night, I found out. I was eating dinner and studying in my favorite restaurant. I was so buried in my studies that I did not notice him sitting across from me. The server came back to my table with my receipt. She told me that the gentlemen at the table across from me took care of it. I looked up, and Dr. Nelson was smiling at me. I got mad as hell.

"You muthafucker!" I thought.

Was he poking fun of me or something? I got up from the table, put some money down for the tip, grabbed my purse, and hurried out the door. By the time I made it to my car, I was in tears.

"What had I done to him?" I wondered.

I sat in my car gathering myself, but the longer I sat, the angrier I became.

"Who did he think he was?" I thought. "He's a professor at the university, and his job is to help his students. I was not going to let him get away with this."

I got out of my car and practically ran back into the restaurant. The hostess recognized me from earlier and asked if I had forgotten something. I ignored him and walked right on in. As I moved closer to his table, I noticed he was signing his receipt. He looked up and handed it back to the server. Our eyes met.

I marched right up to Dr. Nelson's table.

I said, "You won't get away with this. How dare you refuse to help me? Who do you think you are? Then, you try to rub it in my face by paying for my food? Thanks, but no thanks!"

I slapped some money on the table in front of him.

He grabbed my hand and said, "Slow down, Miss. O'Brien. I can explain."

I said, "Get your hands off of me. Explain it to the dean because I will be scheduling a meeting with her first thing tomorrow morning."

By that time, I realized I was causing a scene. Everyone in the restaurant was staring at me.

I said, "Have a great day, Dr. Nelson."

I exited the restaurant. I did not feel as good as I thought I would. I totally embarrassed myself. Once again, by the time I made it back to my car, I was bawling my eyes out.

Someone knocked on my car window. I looked up to see Dr. Nelson. I looked away because I did not want him to see me crying. I started the engine of my car, put it in reverse and lightly pressed the gas pedal.

He begged, "Miss O'Brien, please! Just give me a chance to explain."

I stopped my car, suddenly, probably a little too hard.

I thought to myself, "How in the hell is he going to explain this one?"

He said, "Can you please let down your window? Please, Miss O'Brien, this won't take long. You're right. You deserve an explanation. Give me a chance to give you one."

I put the car in park and let down the window a few inches.

In a sassy tone, I said, "So, now you want to talk because I said I am going to the dean?"

"Miss O'Brien, you have every right to speak to the dean. My job is to teach. I admire your drive to ask for additional assistance when you needed it. So, I don't want you to think for one moment that you did something wrong."

I interrupted, "I know I didn't do anything wrong. You're the one that's wrong."

He continued, "I've regretted saying what I said ever since I said it, especially since I haven't seen you in class anymore. But at the time, I thought I had a good reason for saying it."

I interrupted again, "A good reason! Are you insane? How can you think that you have a good reason for not helping me?"

He sighed. For some reason, it appeared that he was becoming frustrated. This made me feel a little uncomfortable. But, I was able to hold it together because we were in a public place, and I was locked inside my car. If things got bad, I would run the mutherfucker over.

He said through clenched teeth, "Cherry."

That certainly got my attention. He had never called me by my first name before.

"Let me say what I need to say and after that, feel free to go to the dean. You have every reason to. I have been trying to fight this ever since you stepped foot into my class. But things got worse, especially after you started coming to me for tutoring. Although we are both adults, I know I have to hold myself to a higher standard. I've never thought in a million years that this would happen or that these words would come out of my mouth. Miss O'Brien, I can't tutor you anymore because I'm drawn to you."

"Drawn to me?" I questioned. "What does that mean?"

He looked at me like I was crazy or like I was playing.

I guess he realized that I was serious because he said, "Cherry, I cannot tutor you anymore because I am attracted to you, and the thought of us alone is too much for me to handle."

He walked away from my car. I was left speechless.

For the second time in my life, I said, "What the fuck?!?!"

Of course, he did not hear me. He was already in his car by then. On the drive home, I felt cloudy. I could only think about what he said to me.

"Cherry, I cannot tutor you anymore because I am attracted to you, and the thought of us alone in my office is too much for me to handle."

"What the fuck?!" I said again.

When I got back to our apartment, Summer and Aubrey were busy studying, so they didn't realize I was in a trance. Dr. Nelson's words played over and over in my head. Attracted to me? Why? I grabbed my robe and toiletries and headed for the shower.

I questioned myself again, "How can he be attracted to me? Have I done something?"

I turned the shower water to hot and started to undress. When I was completely naked, I looked at myself in the mirror. I got my answer. I saw beauty looking back at me. For the first time, I truly looked at myself. My skin was flawless, sparkling. My teeth were perfect, and lips were plump, tempting. My hair was long and silky, cascading. My eyes were the color of honey, hypnotizing. My breasts were two perfect grapefruits that stood erect, tantalizing. My waist was small and tight, alluring. My hips were curved, captivating. My butt, round and plump, enticing. My thighs were thick, tempting. My body was an hourglass, irresistible. I got in the shower. The hot water felt good. It washed away some of the confusion. I hadn't felt this relaxed in a while. Actually, I hadn't felt this relaxed since being with Braylen. Just the thought of him sent that tingling sensation through my body, a feeling that I had not felt since him. I wanted him. I wanted to feel him again. I closed my eyes and imagined that he was in the shower with me. Oh, how I missed him! His voice, his laughter, his touch, his tongue. I had not been kissed or licked like that in years. As a matter of fact, not since that night. Many guys tried to, but I never allowed any of them. No one except Braylen Miller could say he licked my "honeypot."

I touched myself, imagining that it was Braylen. I was not that sixteen-year-old girl anymore. I was a 20-year-old young lady whose body responded immediately. My nipples became more erect. The heat from the shower water nearly burned my skin, but at the same time, it felt pleasurable. My entire body felt awakened. I welcomed Braylen's touch even more.

I heard him whisper, "Can I lick you, Cherry?"

He would always ask for permission.

"Please, Braylen. I have missed you so much."

I closed my eyes even tighter. My touch felt just like his. I pinched my right nipple with my right hand and rubbed my clit with my left one. My "honeypot" was a pool of moisture, spilling over just for Braylen. Something happened, Braylen disappeared, and Dr. Nelson appeared. I rubbed my clit a little faster.

Dr. Nelson leaned in closer and whispered those words again, "... I am attracted to you, and the thought of us alone is too much for me to handle."

That's all it took. My body exploded. I lost total control. I grabbed the sides of the shower wall to keep from falling. I must have gotten louder than I realized because Summer and Aubrey started banging on the door.

Aubrey said, "Cherry, is everything OK?"

I heard the doorknob rattle. Thank goodness I had locked it. I had to catch my breath before responding.

"I'm fine. Everything's straight."

I heard them walking away from the door. The water began to cool. I reached down to turn it off. I stepped out of the shower and grabbed my towel. I looked at my nakedness once more in the mirror. Beauty stared back, again. I had to gently pat myself dry because my "honeypot" was still pulsating. I slipped on my robe and opened the bathroom door. I grabbed my toiletries and headed into my bedroom. I checked myself in the mirror once more to make sure there was no trace of what just happened. Then, I went to the kitchen to get a glass of water. Summer and Aubrey glanced over at me with accusatory eyes.

I just laughed.

I went back to my room, got under my covers, and closed my eyes. I could not believe what had just happened. In that very moment, it became clear what I needed to do next.

CHAPTER
ELEVEN

Enticed Me

The following Monday, I purposefully arrived to class late. All eyes were on me, including Dr. Nelson's. I wore a button-down, multi-print shirt dress with a red tie around the waist. It hugged all my curves just right. I left the first three buttons undone so my cleavage could peek through. I had on three-inch heels which made the dress appear shorter than it was. I took my seat and crossed my legs. My dress rose a little higher, daring not to expose it all. Dr. Nelson, and some of the other ladies, could not keep their eyes off of me. My lips were shining. With my eyes locked on Dr. Nelson's, I leaned forward just a little so that he could get a better view of my grapefruits. He looked away.

He said, "Class dismissed."

I smirked. I gathered my items, preparing to leave class. Then, accidentally on purpose, my purse tipped over, and all my items spilled out. A classmate rushed over to help, but I refused her help. I bent over to collect my items.

Dr. Nelson stood over me and said, "Miss O'Brien, I see that you have decided to return to class today. Welcome back."

While still bent over, I tilted my head to the side, smiled, bit my bottom lip, and said, "Thanks Dr. Nelson; it's so nice of you to notice my absence."

Quickly, he turned away and headed for the door. Just before reaching it, he stopped.

He said, "You know, Miss O'Brien, I hope you're not toying with me."

I stood up and turned towards him. I straightened my dress and approached him closely. I looked him dead in his eyes and leaned in a little closer, allowing my lips to barely graze his right ear.

I said, "Dr. Nelson, I have no idea what you're talking about? Did I do something wrong? Should I need to report to your office for punishment?"

He closed his eyes and breathed heavily. Automatically, his hand reached for his crouch. Just before grabbing it, he regained his composure. He looked me in the eyes and smiled.

He backed away, walked out the door, and said, "Have a great day, Miss O'Brien!"

AFTER THAT, MY SOLE PURPOSE OF COMING TO CLASS WAS TO seduce Dr. Nelson. A few days later, he asked to see me in his office.

As I stepped into Dr. Nelson's office, I closed the door and took in my surroundings. The space smelled nice, like his cologne, and was impeccably organized. Books lined the shelves, and large windows filled the walls. There was a chaise lounge, two wingback chairs, a desk with a computer and printer, and an office chair. A few pictures hung on the walls, and plants sat on stands, giving the office a touch of warmth, as if it had a woman's influence. I noticed some personal photos on his desk as well.

He invited me to sit, and I accepted. For the first time, I really looked at him. The man was undeniably attractive, and my body responded instantly. As usual, he was dressed sharply in a tailored suit and designer shoes. Dr. Nelson was about six-foot-three, seemed to weigh around 220 pounds, and had a caramel complexion—not too light, not too dark.

"I'm not implying that I prefer one over the other. All shades of black are beautiful to me," I said to Dr. Sartori.

He looked to be in his late forties, with dark brown eyes and salt-and-pepper hair that extended into a neatly groomed mustache and beard. His teeth were flawlessly white. I felt a bit uneasy—not because I thought he'd do anything inappropriate, but because of my own body's reaction to him. My nipples were pressing against my bra, and I think he noticed, as he quickly looked away. It became clear that he felt just as awkward as I did. Dr. Nelson then took a seat.

He started, "Miss O'Brien, I don't think you understand how dangerous this little game is that you are playing, but let me explain it to you. The evening at the restaurant, I tried being honest with you. I recognized that my decision might have been a mistake. I thought that you were mature enough to handle it. Now, I see that you are not. So, let me set the record straight.

I want you to know that you are the only one playing this game. Don't include me in it because I'm not the one to be played with. I am respected in my profession, and I take pride in that. I have never, and don't plan to ever, let anything or anyone get in the way of me doing my job. I have a wife at home and a son that is the same age as you. If I have led you on in any way, I want to apologize. You are a very attractive young lady. Your type of beauty is rare, but I know that you have heard the saying that beauty is only skin deep. You're showing me a side of you that I never want to see again. This show that you are putting on in class is unacceptable, and it stops today. Do I make myself clear?"

I was briefly taken aback. First, because only my brothers, Grandma, Momma, and Daddy had ever spoken to me like that. Second, because I had to admit—it was a bit intimidating. Regaining my composure, I didn't want him to see my momentary vulnerability. I stood up and moved around to his side of the desk, feeling a sense of ease with the blinds closed. Dr. Nelson stayed seated as I stepped to his left, placing the tip of my heel on the armrest of his chair and gently turning him to face me.

I looked him in the eyes and spoke.

"Dr. Nelson, let me make myself clear. You and I can remain respected people and still have fun. So, maybe you should join this game that I'm playing. You have made it clear that you find me attractive; I find you equally attractive. If you are as smart as I think you are, you won't pass up on this opportunity."

I stood between his legs. I raised my dress a little so I could straddle his lap. He attempted to stop me, but not with much force.

I whispered in his ear, "Do you really want me to stop?"

Instead of answering, he grabbed a thigh with each hand. I must admit, it felt good to be touched by him. My breathing increased. I slid up his lap a little further. I locked eyes with him. His hands continued up my thighs. He reached my hips. I raised up to allow him to grab two handfuls.

"Damn, this man smells good!" I thought to myself.

I gently adjusted his head to face me. I bit my bottom lip; he bit his. That was enough. Our lips touched. I licked his bottom lip. Then, we kissed. We kissed and kissed and kissed. His tongue explored my entire mouth and mine did the same to his. I used both of my hands to reach for his desk. I slid my hips on top of it. He stood. I pulled him close. We kissed again. I wrapped my legs around his waist. Our bodies collided. I reached for his belt buckle. He moaned. He grabbed my hands, as if to stop me.

Instead, he started grinding on me, then whispered in my ear, "Please, Miss O'Brien, stop. We should not be doing this."

So, I obeyed. I gently pushed him off of me. Closed my legs. Climbed off his desk. Lowered my skirt.

I said, "Fine, have it your way. But if you change your mind, I think you can use that little computer over there to find my number."

I adjusted myself once more, grabbed my things, and left his office horny as hell.

CHAPTER
TWELVE

Romanced Me

The rest of the week passed in a blur; I couldn't get Dr. Nelson off my mind. I'd tried to tease him, but I think I ended up enticing myself. I did everything I could to keep busy. On Friday night, I hung out with Summer and Aubrey afterward. Saturday morning, we arrived on campus early to host our sorority's Christmas Community Toy Drive. We wanted to make a lot of kids happy on Christmas morning. I was busy sorting toys into boxes with my back to the crowd when I heard a familiar voice behind me.

"Greetings, Sorors. You're doing great work this morning."

It was Dr. Nelson's.

"Thanks, Frat," several Sorors responded in unison.

I turned and our eyes met. I felt so embarrassed, so I turned away from him.

He said, "Hi there, Miss O'Brien. I've left you several voice messages in reference to that project on which we've been working. Can you please return my call as soon as you get the opportunity?"

Wow, I felt incredibly embarrassed at that moment. So embarrassed, I could not speak. Summer nudged my arm.

I stuttered, "Oook, I mean, yes sssssir, I mean, yyyyyes, I will call you sssssir."

He laughed, and so did a few of my Sorors.

He said, "Ladies, keep up the great work, and have a nice day."

I don't think my Sorors picked up on anything between us, because as soon as he walked off, they started giggling and talking about how sexy he was. A few of them joked about the things they would do to him if they got the chance. They just didn't know; I had been thinking the same things.

Eager to hear the message he left on my voicemail, I excused myself and headed towards my car. Once inside, I dialed my voicemail and keyed in my code. I had four new messages.

First message: "Hello, Miss O'Brien. This is Dr. Nelson. Please give me a call at your earliest convenience."

Second message: "Miss O'Brien. This is Dr. Nelson again. I left you a message yesterday. Can you please contact me as soon as possible. My number is 929-443-0937."

I said to Dr. Sartori, "Well, you can probably guess who the third and fourth messages were from."

For some reason, I was too nervous to call him back. His tone had sounded serious. What if he planned to report me to the dean, just like I'd threatened to do to him? I decided not to call him back. I slipped my phone into my purse and returned to the toy drive. We finished up around 8 p.m., and

I told Summer and Aubrey that I'd meet them back at our apartment after grabbing something to eat. As I turned off Spelman Lane, my phone rang. The number 929-443-0937 flashed across the screen, and my heart began to race. I pulled over, hit the button to answer, but although my mouth opened, no words came out.

He said, "So, Miss O'Brien, you finally got around to answering your phone."

I said, "Oh, hello, Dr. Nelson. I did not realize that you called me until you mentioned it this evening."

He laughed. It startled me.

Then he said, "So, you are still playing games, I see!"

I smiled and responded, Dr. Nelson. I'm just waiting for you to make your move. You have to admit that the one I made was one hell of a move."

He laughed again. I laughed too.

He said, "Well, Miss O'Brien, I do believe that I made my move, too, when I called you."

I said, "Really, Dr. Nelson, I hardly call that making a move."

For some reason, his voice was really turning me on.

I continued, "So, according to the rules, it is still your move."

I was the one who laughed first that time.

"So," I continued, "what's your move?"

He asked, "Can you meet me?"

"Meet you? When?"

"Now!" he said, "Meet me now."

I said, "Text me the address, and we'll see what happens."

After that, I hung up the phone. Instantly, a text came through. It was an address; a road I had never heard of before.

"Dang!" I thought. "Am I really going to go through with this?"

Curiosity had gotten the best of me.

I texted back, "See you soon. Send directions not familiar with the address."

I still needed something to eat. I was starving and was starting to feel a little sick. I pulled over at the next fast-food restaurant I saw and ordered fries and a Coke. While waiting on my food, he sent me directions. Dang, this had to be at least a forty-five-minute drive. I wasn't expecting the drive to be that long. Nonetheless, I had nothing else lined up for that night.

As I drove, I tried not to dwell on the decision I was making. My brothers would be so disappointed in me. This man was nearly the same age as my parents. What was I even thinking?

Even so, there was no way I was turning back now, so I pushed those doubts aside. Maybe it was the nerves, but I arrived at the address sooner than expected. A candy apple red Corvette was parked in the driveway, and the house was beautiful—a single-story, vintage-style home made of brick and stone. I checked my reflection in the mirror, freshened up my lipstick, turned off the car, and opened the door. Just as I was about to step out, a wave of uncertainty washed over me. What was I really thinking? I didn't know this place, or who else might be inside. I hesitated, pulling my legs back in and locking the doors.

Just then, the porch light switched on, and the front door opened. Dr. Nelson stepped outside, arms folded, smiling— and looking incredible. My hesitation disappeared as I got out of the car and walked up the driveway toward him.

When I reached the steps, he said, "I was about to win this game after all I see."

I said, "Never doubt a woman on a mission, Dr. Nelson."

He said, "Come on in, Miss O'Brien, we have a lot to talk about."

I asked, "So, I drove this far just to talk?"

He laughed.

I stepped inside of a well-kept home. Someone had a refined sense of style.

I asked, "Whose place is this?"

He answered, "This is my place."

Instantly, I stopped in my tracks. I turned and headed for the door.

"Are you insane inviting me to your home?"

He said, "Woah! Let me explain. This is one of my homes. I rarely come here, but I have someone to check on it often."

I stopped.

"Oh," I said.

He laughed and said, "Well, Miss O'Brien, I think this move just cost you the game."

We both laughed.

He gave me a tour of his home, which looked like something straight out of a magazine. The kitchen was spacious, the four bedrooms were beautifully designed, and the bathrooms were luxurious. The family and dining rooms were equally impressive. After the tour, he invited me back to the family room and offered me some iced tea, but I declined, having just finished a large Coke. Instead, I asked if I could use the bathroom. Once inside, a wave of anxiety hit me, and I took a moment to collect myself. On one hand, my nerves were understandable—I didn't really know much about this man. On the other hand, no one had forced me to come here.

I said to myself, "Get it together, Cherry. You started this game, so let's play it."

After a few minutes, I returned. He had started a fire. It was beautiful. I took a seat on the other side of the room. He laughed. I guess he could sense how nervous I was.

"Miss O'Brien, that little stunt you pulled in my office cannot happen again. Someone could have walked in on us. Do you understand what would have happened?"

I looked down at the floor. I was feeling really bad, actually, ashamed.

He continued, "Then you started showing up in class looking more beautiful than ever. You had to know the effect that would have on me. I wasn't even able to continue with class, and that's not fair to my students, you, or me."

I felt like I was being chastised by my family.

"You really put the icing on the cake with that little stunt you pulled in my office. I've hated myself ever since that happened. How could I allow a student, someone who is young enough to be my daughter, put me in a situation like that? The thought of losing all that I have worked so hard for, my career, my family, and my dignity, makes me realize how reckless I'm capable of being."

And just like that, I found myself in tears. His words cut me like a sword. How could I have been so selfish? So carefree? Grandma didn't raise me like this. I felt like a slut.

He continued, "Miss O'Brien, as much as it kills me to admit this, I have enjoyed every minute of your little game. Like I told you, your beauty is rare; one that is hypnotizing. Not only are you beautiful on the outside, but you also have the intelligence to match it. And for that reason, I can't seem to get you off my mind."

"I know that this could cost me everything, and honestly, I know that I should not be willing to risk it all. I've always been the type of man that played by the rules. I've always been a devoted husband and father. That same devotion has extended itself to my career and my students. So, I have questioned myself over and over again as to why I am willing to risk it all, now."

He took a long pause.

I looked up at him. I didn't expect him to say any of that, or maybe I had heard him wrong.

"What?" I questioned.

He looked me dead in the eyes and said, "I don't know what I'm doing here tonight, or exactly why I invited you here. All I know is that that moment with you made me feel good, and not just sexually. There's something different about you; something I just can't put my finger on. So, I will say this again, I have a lot to lose, Miss O'Brien. If this is just a game for you, end it now. We're at the end of the semester. Christmas break is only a few days away. You'll no longer be my student. All of this can end tonight."

I walked over to his side of the room and sat next to him.

I took his hand and said, "In the beginning this was just a game to me, but I don't think it is anymore. I would love to get to know you better. From your prospective, I may not have as much to lose as you do, but from mine, I do. I, too, am devoted to my family. It would kill them to know that I was here with you tonight. Literally, my brothers would kill you! But, I have to start living my life for me. I have experienced a lot of hurt in my twenty years; hurt from which I may never completely heal. Believe me, I know that THIS is wrong. But sometimes a person gets tired of living up to the standards of others. It is time for me to live for me, Cherry O'Brien."

After that, I reached over and kissed him. He returned the kiss. The passion between us was unimaginable. Finally, we both came up for air.

He stood, reached for my hand, and said, "Come to the kitchen with me. I've ordered dinner."

It was a nice candlelit dinner. We had lamb chops, loaded baked potatoes, asparagus, and pavlova cake for dessert. After dinner, we took a walk around the lake adjacent to his back yard. It was breathtaking. Once we got back to the house, we warmed ourselves in front of the fire. We talked for hours. At around 2 a.m., I heard my phone ring and buzz. I grabbed it out of my purse. It was Summer and Aubrey; they had called and texted umpteen times. I forgot I told them that I was getting something to eat, then coming straight home. I asked Dr. Nelson to excuse me because I needed to make a call. I stepped onto the deck and called Aubrey's phone.

She answered on the first ring.

"Oh, my goodness, Cherry, where are you? Is everything OK? We've been worried sick."

Summer got on the phone next. "Cherry, are you hurt? Where are you?

I said, "Y'all, I'm fine. I lost track of time."

Summer said, "But where are you? Do you know that we were getting ready to call the police? We thought something had happened to you."

I stated, "I'm sorry; I didn't call. But I promise I'm OK. We'll talk once I get home later."

"Later?" Aubrey screamed, "What do you mean by later? Girl, what has gotten into you, or should I say who?"

They both laughed. I laughed, too.

I said, "I will explain everything when I get home. Bye, ladies!"

"Bye, girllllll," they said in unison.

"Don't do anything I would do!" Summer yelled before I hung up.

I laughed again before going back in the house, partly because they were really trippin' and partly because I knew that I could never explain this situation to them.

When I got back inside, Dr. Nelson was still sitting on the sofa waiting for me.

He asked, "Is everything okay?"

"Yes, that was just my roommates checking to make sure everything was OK. I didn't realize that it had gotten so late, but I assured them that everything was going well and that I would be home later."

When I said "later," I realized what that may have implied.

I quickly said, "But I can leave now if you want me too."

He chuckled and said, "Miss O'Brien, I would love for you to spend the night with me."

I smile. He stood and walked over to the fireplace to put it out. Then he left the room and returned with a silk gown.

He said, "I purchased this for you a few days ago."

I laughed and said, "For me? What made you think that you would have the opportunity to give it to me?"

He said, "I kept my fingers crossed."

He escorted me to the master bathroom. He had run a bubble bath.

"Damn!" I thought. "This man had this really figured out!"

It felt good to be treated that way. He told me to relax, and he exited. The water felt good against my skin. I slid down until it reached my chin. I hadn't done that in a long time. After the water turned cold, I stepped out of the tub. I patted myself dry with the towel. I noticed a jar of women's body butter on the counter. I opened the jar; it was unused. I rubbed it all over my body. It had a nice floral smell and felt smooth against my skin. I slipped on the gown. It hugged my curves just right. I exited the bathroom and entered the bedroom. Dr. Nelson was lying on the bed. He smiled at me. I climbed in next to him. He drew me in tightly.

I said, "Dr. Nelson, tonight has been amazing. Thanks for everything."

He said, "First, I need you to stop with Dr. Nelson. My name is William."

"William…" I muttered.

"Oh shit!" I thought to myself, "William?" Why did he have to have the same name as Daddy? Was this a sign; a sign that he was keeping secrets; a sign that he would hurt me?"

I started to feel uncomfortable.

I guess Dr. Nelson, I mean William, sensed my discomfort because he said, "Is everything OK, Miss O'Brien? If you don't feel comfortable calling me William, Dr. Nelson will do."

I said, "No, it's not that. It's just that's my daddy's name, and we don't have a really good relationship. I am fine with calling you William, as long as you call me Cherry."

For some reason, saying the name William brought back so many memories. Those memories made me sad. He held me tight and let the moment pass. He didn't say a word. For the first time, no one wanted to fix things. No one wanted me to talk about it. He just held me and allowed me to work through my emotions in my own way. After about fifteen minutes, he finally spoke.

"Cherry," he said, "thanks for coming tonight. I'm so glad that you are here. This has been just as therapeutic for me as it has been for you. So, thank you."

I looked into his eyes. Mine spoke to him. They told him how much I had enjoyed being here with him, too. I closed my eyes. He started positioning himself on top of me. He kissed my forehead and both of my cheeks. Then, he gently kissed my lips. I could feel myself getting wet and his manhood pressing against me. I opened my eyes so they could tell him that I wanted more. He understood what they were saying and kissed me more passionately. Our tongues intertwined. His mouth was warm and moist. It felt so new, so different. It made me think of Braylen, and I realized that what Braylen and I shared did not compare to what I was feeling at that moment. Instinctively, I began to grind on him. He returned the gesture. It was as if our bodies were in perfect sync. I wrapped my legs around his waist. I wanted to feel more of him. It was so hard. The sensation of it against my "honeypot" was incredibly pleasurable. I had never felt like this before. I could feel myself losing control. My breathing became heavier.

Just when it was about to happen, he whispered, "Are you OK, Cherry?"

I said, "Yes, it just feels so good." He rolled over.

I asked, "Did I say something wrong?"

He said, "Cherry, I have to ask you a question."

I positioned myself on top of him and whispered back, "We can talk later."

He said, "No, Cherry, I have to ask you something, some-thing important."

He was definitely killing the mood. I could tell by the way he spoke that it was something serious, though.

I got off of him, sat up on the bed, and asked, "What's wrong?"

He laughed and said, "Nothing is wrong. I just need to ask you something. Have you ever done this before?"

Embarrassed, I looked away from him and asked, "What do you mean? Done what?"

He said, "I think you know exactly what I mean. Have you ever had sex before?"

Still embarrassed, I said, "No, you can tell?"

Hugged me and kissed me gently on the neck.

He said, "Like I told you before, Cherry, a beauty like yours is rare. So, something in my gut just told me, but I want-ed to be sure. You are special and what we got here can be just as special. As much as I want you right now, I cannot do this. I want you to be sure.

Too excited, I said, "I'm sure!"

He said, "Cherry, I know your body is sure, but I want your mind and heart to be sure, too. We have no reason to rush this. I don't want you to have any regrets. So, I tell you what, Christmas break is just four days away. Are you plan-ning to travel home?"

I answered, "Yes."

"Go home to your family. Spend time with them. Enjoy the holidays. Afterwards, if you still want me, I'll be waiting. But, if you have second thoughts, any whatsoever, I don't want you to hesitate to tell me. We will go on with our lives as if none of this ever happened. Do we have an agreement?"

I nodded in agreement.

He hugged me a little tighter. He smelled so damn good!

"Boy," I thought to myself, "this is going to be one long ass night."

But it wasn't. We spent the rest of the night talking and laughing. I don't even remember falling asleep.

CHAPTER
THIRTEEN

Assured Me

My phone started buzzing. I reached for it off the nightstand. The caller ID told me it was Grandma. I slid out of bed and tip-toed into the bathroom.

Once inside, I answered, "Hey, Grandma, is everything OK?"

She said, "What do you mean, child? Does something have to be wrong for me to call you? I just miss you, that's all."

I said, "I miss you, too, Grandma."

She continued, "I'm just excited because my baby is coming home in a few days. I haven't seen you in months. We're all excited."

"We?" I questioned.

Greyson and Sterling screamed through the phone, "Hey, Riri, we miss you."

I said, "I miss y'all, too."

"What are you doing?" Sterling asked. "Where's Summer and Aubrey?"

I didn't want to lie to them, so, I said, "Do y'all know how early it is?"

Greyson said, "Early! Girl, what are you talking about? It is two o'clock in the afternoon."

"Two o'clock? "I questioned.

He said, "Yeah, Little Sis, don't tell me you partied that hard last night?!?"

At that point I don't remember much of anything else they said. I was thinking about the night before and the gorgeous man I spent it with.

I was brought back to reality when I heard Greyson say, "Cherry, are you still there?"

"Oh, yeah," I stammered, "I'm still here."

He continued, "We can't wait to see you in a few days, Sis. Take care, get some rest, and we will pick you up from the airport on Wednesday."

We said our goodbyes, and I ended the call.

William came to the bathroom door and asked, "Is everything OK, Cherry?"

I opened it and said, "Yes, everything is fine. That was my grandma and brothers calling to check on me. They're excited about me coming home for the break."

William pulled me close to him and hugged me tight. It felt good to be in his arms again.

He said, "You know, I don't know much about your family. Maybe you can tell me about them over brunch."

"Brunch?" I asked, "I thought maybe I could be your brunch?"

He said, "Slow down, Miss Cherry O'Brien. We have plenty of time for that. Remember our agreement!"

Those were not the words for which I was hoping. He excused himself into the bathroom. While there, I sent Summer and Aubrey a quick text to let them know I was fine and would be home in a few hours. I placed my phone back on the nightstand. Instantly, it started going off. I did not have to look at it to know who it was. I giggled to myself.

Together, we prepared a lovely brunch of chicken and red velvet waffle kabobs, shrimp and grits, bruschetta, mini crab cakes, and fresh fruit. The table was set with fresh flowers and candles, creating a warm atmosphere as we chatted and laughed. He asked about my family again, so I shared only what I wanted him to know. I told him I had a momma and daddy, but that my grandma was the one who raised me. I sensed he wanted to ask more about that, but he didn't press. I talked about my older brothers and how they moved to Texas during my junior year of high school to be closer to me, and I shared how much I adored Lavender. For some reason, though, I didn't mention Olivia or Lisa. My phone continued to ping. I explained that the texts were from my childhood best friends, Summer and Aubrey, who weren't used to me staying out overnight.

He smiled and said, "Well, that is good to know."

After that, he opened up about his family. He'd been married to his wife for over twenty years, and they had one son, Landon, who was twenty and attended Morehouse College.

As if reading my mind, he said, "That's part of what makes this so difficult. My son could be—or rather, should be—the one sitting here with you instead of me."

He also told me that his wife was a wonderful mother. Though they had their share of disagreements, she would never suspect him of something like this.

I lowered my head, feeling a wave of guilt. Hearing him say that made me question myself. Was I more like my parents than I wanted to admit? I felt a strong attraction to Dr. Nelson, and I wondered if this had been the same irresistible pull my parents had once felt for each other.

Sensing my unease, Dr. Nelson stood up, took my hand, pulled me close, and kissed me. His kisses were intoxicating—like a drug my body was starting to crave, an art form in themselves. My breathing quickened as my hands began to explore his body, feeling his strength. His arousal pressed against my stomach, and with each kiss, my desire grew. I wanted him as much as he wanted me. He lifted me up, and I wrapped my legs around his waist as he carried me to the bedroom. He gently laid me down on the bed, pulled off his T-shirt, revealing his sculpted, muscular body. I smiled, showing my approval. He then slipped out of his pants; his arousal clearly visible beneath his boxers. He lay down over me, raising my gown, and then kissed my inner thigh.

I closed my eyes and begged, "Please!"

With my panties still on, he used his finger to rub my clit. His touch made me wet and moan. His breathing started to increase. He slid down and kissed my clit through my panties then traveled up my body with small kisses. When he reached my lips, our eyes met. Our passion increased. Our tongues danced. He tugged on my bottom lip. I locked my legs around his waist. I decided then and there that I wanted him inside of me. I used my right hand to tug at his boxers. I loosened my legs to free him, hoping he would remove his boxers, hoping he understood what I wanted. Instead, he got up.

He said, "Cherry, I'm serious, we can't do this right now. We have to wait."

He sat on the bed.

He patted on it with his hand and said, "Cherry, sit with me."

I hesitated, but I did as he asked.

He continued, "Cherry, do you understand how much more complicated this thing can get? Like I said yesterday, I can't let you do something that you may regret later."

I interrupted, "But I won't regret it. I want to do this."

He said, "But, I will feel better once you have had time to think about it. You've already waited twenty years. I don't want you to get caught up in the moment and make a hasty decision. Although your body is saying yes, I want your mind and heart to do the same. I want you to understand the possible risks and consequences. I want you to be 100 percent sure about this. There are some young men your age that deserve you. I have done things and experienced things that you have yet to experience. I would never want to take something from you that is as precious as your virginity if you are not completely sure that I deserve it. In fact, I can tell you that I don't. I have a wife and a son. So, Cherry, realize that I can never be the person that you deserve. You deserve someone that can be fully committed to you, not someone who has to lie to his family just to get to see you, just to get to talk to you, just to get to touch you. You deserve someone that can give you the life that you deserve. The life that I already have. You deserve a man who can fully commit to you. I'm not that person. So, I want you to take all the time you need before making this decision.

I don't want you to regret it. I can assure you, if I'm the one you want, I will be here waiting when you return."

I am not sure when it happened. Unsurprisingly, I ended up in tears. I was crying for two reasons. The first reason was because I knew all the things he was saying were true. I needed to be sure I was making the right decision. Grandma always instilled in me that my body was sacred. I should cherish it and never let anyone dip into my "honeypot" unless it was my husband. The second reason I was crying was because at that very moment, Dr. Nelson's words touched me. They made me feel special. And I was sure that he was the one I wanted.

After our talk, we showered, separately of course, and spent the rest of the evening together. Around six o'clock, I was tired of Summer and Aubrey calling and texting, so we kissed and said our goodbyes.

About five minutes down the road, I received a text. I was expecting it to be from Aubrey or Summer. Instead, it was from Dr. Nelson. He sent me three simple words that made me realize that he was the one.

They read, "Miss you already."

CHAPTER
FOURTEEN

Hurt Me

"Alright Dr. Sartori, let's fast-forward to Winter Break. Everything went well back home. Truthfully, it felt amazing to be with my family. Momma and Lavender spent Christmas break with us. Grandma prepared a southern Christmas dinner that consisted of honey-chipotle glazed turkey, pineapple-baked ham with brown sugar glaze, honey-glazed BBQ ribs, southern fried chicken, bacon-wrapped filets with cowboy butter, cornbread dressing, giblet gravy, homemade cranberry sauce, buttermilk mashed potatoes, deviled eggs, creamy potato salad, bacon-wrapped asparagus, maple-bacon brussels sprouts, ham-hock collard greens, country green beans, lima beans, freshly stewed corn, butternut squash casserole, cheesy broccoli and rice casserole, five-cheese macaroni and cheese, creamy chicken pot pie, skillet dinner rolls with garlic-herb butter, old-fashioned candied yams, sweet potato pie, sweet potato casserole, pecan pie, dreamy white Christmas cake, cream cheese pound cake, red velvet cake, fresh coconut cake, sweet tea, lemonade, fruit punch, and soda. After eating, we were instantly put in a food coma."

We exchanged gifts and spent the entire Winter Break together. Daddy, Lisa, and Olivia called to wish everyone a Merry Christmas. I received a Holiday card with a personal check in the mail from the Millers. Dr. Sartori looked puzzled.

So, I said, "Dr. Sartori, The Millers were still feeling guilty, and the gifts were still coming."

A peculiar incident occurred during the break. As a matter of fact, it was on Christmas Day. My brothers and I were walking out of the front door. I was just about to get in Sterling's car. When I looked up, I could have sworn I saw Braylen drive by the house. I assumed I was imagining things, yet a part of me kept insisting it was actually him. In the following days, I drove pass the Miller's house repeatedly, but there was no indication that Braylen was around.

For New Year's, Grandma prepared another southern tradition, collard greens, black-eyed peas, cornbread, and fried chicken. It was believed that eating those foods symbolized fortune in the forthcoming year. The peas represented coins, while the collard greens represented paper money. The cornbread represented gold. The chicken was just good ole eating.

Although Winter Break was great, I often found myself thinking of Dr. Nelson. I considered giving him a call, but I figured he was spending time with his family and didn't want to chance his wife answering the phone. I decided to do something else instead; I did a Google search of his name, and, surprisingly, I learned a great deal. As he mentioned, he had a wife and one child. There was a photograph of the three of them. His wife was drop-dead gorgeous; and their son was a combination of them both. Dr. Nelson was only a part time professor at the university. His full-time job was somewhat of an engineering expert. He was a consultant for several major engineering companies across the country. He had published several scholarly journals, articles, and books on engineering. He traveled all around the world consulting and conferencing on design processes and failures, fundamental principles, and the history and nature of engineering. Basically, he was an expert on the ABCs and 123s of engineering.

"Wow!" I said aloud, "This explains a lot; he's paid!"

The remainder of Winter Break flew by. I was glad because I couldn't get Dr. Nelson off my mind. He had so much more to offer me than just his heart, if you know what I mean. I didn't feel too optimistic about my future with Dr. Nelson. What if he didn't want me anymore? What if his conscience bothered him, and he reconsidered? What if he was lying to me and had done this to others before me? What if I wasn't the only one he was currently lying to? What if he's a killer or rapist or something? The longer I stayed in Texas, the more I realized that maybe he was fooling me. But for some strange reason, even with those thoughts, I still missed him. I had never spent a romantic day, let alone, a night with a man before, and I wanted more of that.

When it was time for Summer, Aubrey, and me to head to the airport for our flight back to Georgia, I felt a mix of relief and nervousness. Summer and Aubrey noticed.

Summer jokingly said, "It looks like somebody got a lot on her mind. I guess she is ready to get back to Atlanta to see this mystery man she hasn't told us about."

Aubrey added, "Yeah, the one we can't get any info on."

I smiled. I didn't tell them about Dr. Nelson. Instead, I made up a lie about a guy that I met at Morehouse. Because I wasn't sure if things were going to get serious or not, I wanted to see where it was going before I introduced them to him. With Summer being Summer, she wanted to know if I gave up the "honeypot." I assured her that I didn't. From there, they just reminded me of the importance of being careful since I wasn't willing to let them know who he was. I assured them that I understood. The world is crazy, and full of people that do crazy shit.

When we arrived at our apartment on Saturday, we were thankful for the quietness. The holidays were so busy, so we needed some well-deserved rest. We slept the remainder of the day and felt totally refreshed when we woke up Sunday morning. By Sunday, I was ready to hear from Dr. Nelson, but I didn't want to seem too desperate by calling him. He didn't call me either.

When classes started that week, I looked for him around campus, but he was nowhere to be found. I would purposefully walk by his office, but there were no signs of him. I even drove by his house, but I saw no signs of life. By Thursday, I was furious with myself for allowing Dr. Nelson to get to me. He totally used me! But for what? We did not have sex, so what had he used me for? Maybe he was planning to blackmail me or something. Did he take pictures of me while I was bathing or sleeping? Maybe he had something else on me. Did the Millers put him up to it? But, that didn't make sense, because they would have more to lose if people found out what their son did to me.

By the end of the week, I decided I needed to put Dr. Nelson out of my mind for good. I needed to forget what happened between us and how special he made me feel. That meant one thing and one thing only: time with my Sorors in the ATL.

Nightlife in Atlanta was filled with good vibes, laughter, music, people, dancing, eating, and drinking. We went to one of the local clubs. I spent most of the night dancing with this fine ass Alpha from Morehouse. He was just what I needed to get my mind off of Dr. Nelson. Plus, he was the perfect ploy to fool Summer and Aubrey. The way he and I were dancing, laughing, and getting close made them assume he was the mystery man I had been seeing before Winter Break. By the time Summer, Aubrey, and I left the club early Sunday morning, we were hot, tired, sweaty, hungry, and ready for a shower and the bed. We slept the entire day away. Before I knew it, it was Monday morning.

I hit the snooze button a few times, then dragged myself into the shower. The water felt amazing as it ran down my body, but I had to rush through my shower, get dressed, throw my hair into a ponytail, grab a piece of fruit, and head out the door to make it on time to my 9am class. I hated being late for classes because I took my education seriously. I had clear life goals, and I wasn't going to let anything—or anyone—stand in the way of achieving them.

I made it to class on time, and as I settled into my seat, I thought I saw Dr. Nelson walk by. I figured my eyes must have been playing tricks on me, since his office and classes were on the third floor, while all of mine were on the fifth. I couldn't help but wonder why he would be on the fifth floor if he didn't have a reason to be there. Curiosity got the best of me. I collected my purse and other items, and I headed for the door. As soon as I stepped outside the classroom, I thought I saw him turn the corner. I quickened my pace. As I turned the corner, I spotted the person stepping onto the elevator. It felt like I was in a scene from a horror or mystery movie, chasing a madman who might turn around and stab me at any moment. My heart pounded so hard that I could hear it ringing in my ears. I was incredibly nervous. Once I reached the elevator, I pressed the down button. I waited and waited. I couldn't wait any longer, so I decided to hit the stairs. When I entered the stairwell, I began to feel foolish. What was I thinking, leaving class because I thought I saw Dr. Nelson? Was I losing my mind? First, it was Braylen riding by Grandma's house. Now, it's Dr. Nelson walking by the classroom. Those thoughts caused me to slow down a bit. When I exited the stairwell, something made me realize that I wasn't losing my mind. It was Dr. Nelson's laugh. It's very distinct. I rounded the corner and saw him laughing with another professor. My eyes locked with his. I wanted to glare a hole right through him. The other professor noticed Dr. Nelson staring at something, so he turned to see what had caught Dr. Nelson's attention. I walked closer to them, clenching my fists, gritting my teeth, and rolling my eyes.

I was about to say something, when the other professor said, "Hey, how are you today, young lady?"

I said, "Couldn't be better, Sir!"

I kept walking. I was glad to get to the end of the hall and turn the corner. I was crying. "How could he do this to me?," I thought. I guess he was playing the game and winning! I re-entered the stairwell and hurried down to the first floor. By the time I left the building, I felt myself spinning out of control. I was shaking with a mix of hurt and anger.

I hurried to my car. My cell phone began ringing. I ignored the call; it started buzzing with text messages, which I also ignored.

I sat in my car, trying to gather my thoughts until it was time for my next class because, as I mentioned earlier, "Nothing and no one will stand in the way of me achieving my goals."

I took a deep breath and went back inside. I got on the elevator; it was pretty full as usual. The button for the fifth floor was already lit. I stepped off with reassurance and convinced myself that I could handle anything that came my way. I smoothed my dress and walked down the hall with the confidence Grandma instilled in me. That same confidence left when I turned the corner. There, leaning against the wall, was Dr. Nelson. I tried to turn around before he saw me, but it was too late. He started walking straight toward me, and I froze. Someone bumped into me, making me stumble. Dr. Nelson approached and stopped directly in front of me.

He said, "Good afternoon, Miss O'Brien. I was just looking for you. Can I see you in my office for a moment?"

I nodded. We got onto the elevator, which was still full. He pushed the button for the third floor. I was beginning to get upset again. Once we reached the third floor, we stepped off the elevator and headed towards his office. I could feel my heart pounding again; it was so intense that I thought I might hyperventilate. I was more frustrated with myself for letting him get to me. I stopped walking, and he seemed to sense it, as he paused too.

He turned around and said, "Is everything okay, Miss O'Brien? My office is just around this corner. This will only take a second."

I didn't move.

He said, "Miss O'Brien, please follow me. I promise I won't take up too much of your time."

I noticed that familiar smirk forming at the corner of his mouth, and it gave me the motivation I needed to keep moving. He was trying to make a fool of me! I couldn't reach his office fast enough. I was furious.

When we arrived, Dr. Nelson opened the door and let me enter first. He closed the door and took a seat in his office chair. Once inside, my eyes fell on his desk, and I remembered our escapade on it. The idea of his lips on mine sent a tingle through me, but I quickly composed myself, afraid to reveal any signs of weakness.

Standing at the door with my arms crossed, I spoke.

"You wanted to see me, Dr. Nelson?" I asked.

He smiled the smile I loved to see.

He chuckled and said, "Oh, I guess we are back to last-name basis; what ever happened to William?"

I put my right hand on my hip and said sharply, "William was this nice guy I spent some time with a couple weeks ago. I haven't seen nor heard from him since then.

So, I'll ask again, did you need to see me Dr. Nelson?"

He stood and started walking towards me. I put my left hand on the doorknob, threatening to leave. He stopped.

He said, "Miss O'Brien, there has been a huge misunderstanding."

I interrupted, "Nope, not a misunderstanding at all, Dr. Nelson. It is perfectly clear where we stand."

He started moving closer again. I turned the doorknob. He stopped again.

He said, "Cherry–"

I interjected, "It's Miss O'Brien!"

He continued, "Miss O'Brien, I can assure you that there has been a misunderstanding…."

Before he could go on, there was a knock on the door that nearly startled me. I opened it to find Dr. Mitchell on the other side.

She said, "Oh, I'm so sorry to interrupt, Dr. Nelson. I didn't realize that you had someone with you. I'll come back later."

Dr. Nelson said, "OK, thanks."

This was my opportunity to escape.

I said, "Oh, you're fine, Dr. Mitchell. Dr. Nelson and I were just finishing up. I'm actually leaving."

I hurried out the door, feeling a sudden wave of embarrassment and shame. However, the more I walked away from his office, the more upset I became. When I turned the corner and spotted an empty classroom, I felt a sense of relief. I stepped inside and closed the door behind me, sliding down to the floor as tears streamed down my face. I cried for the pain that the men in my life caused. The pain I endured from Daddy and my brothers, the loss of Braylen, and finally, for the pain caused by another man: Dr. Nelson.

CHAPTER
FIFTEEN

Apologized To Me

I composed myself, stood up with the confidence and grace that Grandma had instilled in me, and left the classroom. I tugged slightly on my dress and headed to classes. The remainder of them flew by. I was exhausted by the time I got back to my apartment. Summer and Aubrey were in class, so I was glad to have the place to myself. I grabbed some milk out of the fridge, heated it, and added cocoa powder. It warmed my body perfectly. I headed for my bedroom, sat in my recliner, and grabbed my phone from my purse. There were twenty-seven missed calls, thirteen voice messages, and fifteen texts. My heart leaped into my throat, and I felt a wave of panic. All of the messages were from Dr. Nelson. I clicked on the messages and began reading them.

Message 1: Miss O'Brien, please give me a call as soon as you get this message.

Message 2: Miss O'Brien, I really need to hear from you soon. It's urgent.

Message 3: Miss O'Brien, this is Dr. Nelson, I need to speak with you concerning an urgent matter.

Message 4: Cherry, please call me.

Message 5: Cherry, what I have to say maybe worth hearing. Call me.

Message 6: Please don't do this to me. Just call me. I can explain.

Message 7: Cherry, please.

After the seventh message, I had read enough. I couldn't take any more of his begging and lies. I deleted the rest of the messages without reading them. I stepped into my bathroom to run a bath. I got undressed, turned on some R&B music and eased into the bathtub. The water was hot, almost too hot. It felt good, and I needed to relax. I tried to forget about William, but it was hard. What kind of explanation could he possibly have? What kind of game was he playing? Why did I put myself in these situations to be continuously hurt by men? I wanted answers, but I didn't have the mental strength to deal with William and his lies.

After a while, I heard Aubrey and Summer come through the front door. They were bustling around in the kitchen, likely starting dinner. My bath water was starting to feel cool, so I got out of the tub. I dried myself off then applied my favorite body butter. I slipped on some panties, an oversized t-shirt, and slippers. I opened my bedroom door and headed to the kitchen.

"Hey, y'all!"

Aubrey said, "Girl, I was just telling Summer about this fine ass brother I met from Morehouse. I was jogging in the park, and I stopped to check my heartrate. Coincidentally, he was doing the same. We made eye contact, so he walked over and introduced himself. Y'all, I could barely think straight; he's so fine. We exchanged numbers and made plans to see each other this weekend."

I said, "Go, You!"

She went on to say that they finished their jog together then went to the local juice bar for a smoothie. There was instant chemistry.

I had to admit, I had not seen Aubrey that excited about someone since, well, I couldn't remember the last time. Thinking about her happiness brought back memories of my own times of joy. My mind wandered back to my childhood, a time when everything felt simple, before I discovered the secret my family had kept from me. My thoughts shifted to Braylen. I can genuinely say that I was truly content when he was in my life—he always knew how to make me laugh. He wiped away my tears and made me forget about the loneliness of being a part from my parents and brothers. He made me feel special—not just in a physical sense, but like he truly saw me for who I was, beyond just a pretty face and curves. Next, my thoughts turned to Dr Nelson. With him, I experienced something entirely new. He always knew exactly what to say, how to say it, and when to say it. I adored his smile, his laughter, and the way he crafted his words. He made me feel cherished without even touching me. I admired his maturity, his wisdom, his cooking, his taste in music, movies, and even his sense of decor.

Aubrey and Summer realized my thoughts had drifted elsewhere, because they both yelled my name and waved their hands in front of my face.

"Earth to Riri," Aubrey said, "Is everything OK?"

"Yeah," I said, "I was just thinking about something."

Summer said, "Or were you thinking about someone?"

They both giggled.

Aubrey said, "Come on, Riri, tell us about your mystery man."

I said, "This conversation is not about me. We're talking about you and your Morehouse man."

She said, "Oh, I'm definitely not keeping him a secret. His name is Landon Nelson."

Summer and I looked at each other as if that name was supposed to mean something to us.

Aubrey said, "Come on, girls, you know who I'm talking about—Landon Nelson. He's Dr. Nelson's son, the professor who works at Spelman."

My jaw dropped.

"Whose son!?" I asked, a little too interested.

Both Aubrey and Summer looked at me.

"Damn," Aubrey said. "Do you know him or know something about him that I should know?"

"Girl, no, but if he looks anything like his sexy ass daddy, then, honey, I know he's fine," I said, trying to cover my guilt.

Hearing Dr. Nelson's name stirred up memories I was desperately trying to bury. Deep down, it affected me, though neither Summer nor Aubrey seemed to notice my unease. The conversation carried on, but my interest faded. My thoughts were consumed by memories of Dr. Nelson, the way he made me feel, and my longing to experience that feeling again.

We spent the rest of the night talking, laughing, eating popcorn, and watching movies. It felt great to have some quality time with them. When morning arrived, I felt stiff and a bit trapped from falling asleep on the sofa with Summer and Aubrey. As I tried to wiggle my way out from between them, they stirred as well.

"Dang," Summer said sleepily, "I feel like I just been hit by a car. Y'all sleep too wild for me."

Aubrey responded cheerfully, "Summer, it's not us. This sofa isn't made for three people to sleep on. We better get moving. We have our annual voter registration starts in an hour. Let's get dressed and head to campus.

Summer said, "Aubrey, girl, don't play us like you are 'Miss Bright and Early.' You're just excited to be somewhere on time for once because you're hoping to see Landon Nelson."

The thought of the name Nelson sent my stomach in knots.

I said, "Excuse me, y'all. My stomach is turning somersaults. I got to go to the bathroom, now!" They both laughed but quickly moved out of my way.

When I got to the bathroom, I looked at myself in the mirror and said aloud, "Cherry, get your act together. You spent one night with this man, and you are acting like it was an eternity. Y'all kissed, had dinner, talked, and that's it. Get over William Nelson!"

I stepped out of the bathroom with a new zest of confidence. However, it did not last too long.

We were dressed and out of the door within the hour. Once we arrived on campus, it was clear to us that it would be a successful community event. People were waiting in line to register and volunteer in some fashion. Food trucks lined the street, and a local DJ had the crowd jumping. It felt good to see people working together for such a great cause. Eyeing the crowd, I saw many familiar faces, but there was one I was looking for in particular: Dr. Nelson's. I was relieved when I did not see it. That meant that I could put in work without him being a distraction.

Time flew by. Before I knew it, it was 3 p.m. My stomach was begging for food. As if on cue, Summer, Aubrey, and I made eye contact. We were all thinking the same thing and headed in the direction of the food trucks. There were plenty of choices, but we were looking for one in particular. When we spotted it, we knew exactly what time it was. The line was long, but we knew it would be worth the wait. While in line, we chatted about the success of the event and admired our sorority's focus on serving the community. We were dedicated to its purpose and oath, and thankful for our founders who paved the way. This was a lifetime commitment that we took seriously. My Sorors were my family. We crossed the burning sands together. We laughed together. We cried together. We studied together. We prayed together. We served together. We worshiped together. We ate together. We partied together. Most importantly, we loved, respected, and cherished each other.

When we finally reached the front of the line, Summer ordered our favorites: seafood fries, with extra sauce, mini tacos, and freshly-squeezed lemonade.

Summer reached into her purse for some cash when a familiar voice said, "Good afternoon, ladies. It would be my pleasure to take care of this for you."

I turned around and locked eyes with Dr. Nelson and Landon. He caught me off guard because I was convinced he wasn't.

I said, "That's OK, Dr. Nelson, I got it."

I pushed my way in front of Summer while digging in my purse.

He stepped directly behind me and said, "Miss O'Brien, it really would be my pleasure."

He emphasized the words 'my pleasure.'

"You deserve it after such a successful event y'all put together today."

Before I could interject again, he reached over my shoulder and handed the cashier the money. I did not say anything else. Landon had totally stolen Aubrey and Summer's attention, so that left me standing with Dr. Nelson. We were just standing there looking at each other. I wanted him to walk away, or I thought I did.

He whispered, "Cherry, why haven't you returned any of my calls? What's going on?"

I crossed my arms and just ignored his questions.

He continued, "We need to talk. I can explain everything. Just give me a chance."

I was just getting ready to respond when our order number was called. Thankful was an understatement. Summer, Aubrey, and I eased back to the front of the line to grab our food. Summer and Aubrey thanked Dr. Nelson, but I simply walked away. Why did I have to thank him? Playing me? Romancing me? Leading me on? Making me love him? Humiliating me? Making me question my decisions?

We moved to an area of campus that was a little less crowded to eat our food. It was to die for. The seafood fries were made of fresh cut potatoes topped with crab and lobster meat, sauteed shrimp, onions, and bell peppers, and drizzled with a creamy sauce. The mini tacos were seasoned with pork and the perfect balance of spicy and sweet. The freshly-squeezed lemonade had the perfect balance of sweet and sour.

After that, we decided to mingle. As we walked through the crowds, I noticed that Dr. Nelson could not keep his eyes off of me, so I gave him something to look at. My Sorors and I, as well as other sororities and fraternities, strolled to various songs. I made sure to roll and shake my body a little harder than usual. The DJ had us crunk. He took us back. The self-made dance floor got crowded. Bodies were dancing, bumping, grinding, swaying, popping, and gyrating. Still, Dr. Nelson had his eyes locked on me. I grabbed Terrance, a fine-ass Omega, by the hand and led him to the dance floor. Terrance and I had gone out a few times. He had a serious crush on me, but I wasn't ready to have the type of relationship that he wanted. He wanted us to be exclusive, and I wasn't interested. I wasn't ready to be locked in with one guy, not that I wanted more than one. No, that wasn't it at all. I just didn't want to be locked down with anyone. I had seen that too many times with Summer and Aubrey, and it never ended well. It always ended with a lot of arguing and other bullshit that I did not need in my life. My focus was on school and that was enough to keep me occupied. Anyways, Terrance and I left everything we had on the dance floor. He was rubbing all over my body and his grind was intense. I must admit, it felt good. But, I had one mission: to make Dr. Nelson jealous and make him realize that he made a mistake by playing with me. Terrance's erection was poking me. I was grinding on that thing so hard that it almost felt like we were fucking with our clothes on. My eyes stayed on Dr. Nelson the entire time, and his eyes dared not leave Terrence and me. I could tell that he hated the way Terrance was feeling all over my body, so I allowed him to feel way more than usual. After a few songs, he couldn't resist any longer. He leaned down and planted a kiss on the side of my neck.

He whispered in my ear, "Can we go somewhere and talk?"

"Talk," I laughed to myself. "Talking was the last thing on his mind," I thought.

To avoid completely hurting his feelings, I whispered back, "Maybe next time."

I led him off the dance floor. I purposefully led him out of Dr. Nelson's sight to make him wonder where we were going.

I said, "I'm sorry if I gave you the wrong impression. You're a really nice guy, but I'm still not ready to become anything more than friends."

The look on his face was disappointing yet understanding, but the erection in his pants was still pleading.

He said, "Please, Cherry, we don't have to do anything. Just give me the opportunity to get to know you a little better. No strings attached."

I said, "Maybe another time, Terrance. I'm really tired."

I glanced at his manhood and remarked, "Besides, I think he has more than just getting to know me on his mind."

I left him and his erection, just standing there. I got in my car and took a deep breath. I closed my eyes and rested my head on the steering wheel. I felt horrible for using Terrance. I was getting ready to put my key in the ignition when I heard a knock on my window.

I mumbled, "Fuck, not Terrance, again!"

I lifted my head off the steering wheel. It was not Terrance. It was Dr. Nelson.

I yelled, "Are you serious? Have you lost your mind? Someone may see you!"

He said, "Well, in that case, open your door so I can get in. We need to talk."

I put my key in the ignition.

He pleaded, "Cherry, please, just give me five minutes. After that, you can walk away, and I won't bother you again."

I slowly slid my finger to the automatic button and pressed unlock. He hurried to the passenger side, carefully looking to make sure no one saw him getting in.

He closed the door and said, "Cherry, how have you been?"

I looked at him and firmly said, "You have five minutes. Make them count."

He began. "You did not hear from me after Winter Break, but I can explain."

I guess he expected me to say something, but I just stared into his eyes waiting for him to continue.

He told me that during Christmas, he traveled to California with his wife and son for a speaking engagement. Initially, his family was planning to attend, but at the last minute, they decided to join him. After the conference, they spent an extra week in California, just to relax and get away from the stress of work and life.

I looked at him as if he was telling a bold-faced lie.

He claimed that he wanted to reach out to me, but it wasn't possible because they spent all of their time together. When I saw him on campus, he had just returned to Atlanta the night before.

I sucked my teeth to let him know that I wasn't believing him.

But, he said something to make me think he may have not been lying.

"Like I've said before, Cherry, you are a very special young lady, and I would never do anything to deliberately hurt, mislead, or deceive you. I missed you like crazy. I was ecstatic when I finally saw you on campus. I wanted to run to you and hold you in my arms, but the look on your face told me that you didn't want the same. At first, I assumed you were upset with me for staying out of town longer than anticipated. Then, I wondered if, after some time apart, you concluded that it would be best for us not to get involved with each other.

I convinced myself that I was going to just forget about the night I spent with you, but today when I saw you at the drive, I could not keep my eyes off of you. I offered to pay for your lunch because I wanted to be close to you. I wanted you to look into my eyes to see that I am sorry. I wanted to know that maybe there was a chance for us. I saw you and that young man dancing. He was touching on you and enjoying himself. Then, y'all left. You don't want to know what my mind told me y'all were leaving to do. I don't mean that in a disrespectful way. You're a jewel; any man would be lucky to have you. I got jealous and followed you. Do you know how relieved I was to see the two of you go your separate ways? I saw you sitting alone in your car, I just had to come over. I thought that this was my opportunity to tell you my side of the story; my last opportunity to make things right with you. I'm hoping that you are willing to give me the opportunity to make it up to you. Cherry, I know that I'm married, and this makes everything I'm saying wrong, but that doesn't change the way I feel about you. I want to give you and show you the world."

He finally stopped talking and took a deep breath. We looked at each other. I think I saw a tear form in the corner of in his eye.

He spoke again, "Please say something, Cherry. Even if it's not what I want to hear, just say something."

I said, "Your five minutes were up about three minutes ago."

He said, "I'm sorry to have wasted your time, Miss O'Brien."

He placed his hand on the door to open it. I placed my right hand on his left knee and smiled.

I said, "I missed you, too, Dr. Nelson. I'm glad you didn't give up on me."

Afterwards, he did something that I hadn't expected but wanted and missed so badly. He cupped my face in his hand and kissed me.

The kiss was filled with passion. I moaned. I think that moan brought him back to reality because he quickly pulled away. My eyes were still closed because I wanted more. He chuckled, the chuckle that I missed hearing. I opened my eyes. We looked at each other.

He asked, "When can I see you?"

I smiled.

He continued, "Before you say something smart, I mean see you to make up for this misunderstanding."

I asked, "How about this coming Friday?"

He said, "Friday night can't come fast enough."

He opened the door, turned to me, and said, "Cherry, I really did miss you. Do me a favor, the next time I call or text you, please respond. Don't punish me like that anymore."

I said, "I won't, and I can't wait to see you again, William."

CHAPTER
SIXTEEN

Schooled Me

By the time I pulled into my apartment complex, I was on cloud nine. I had spent one sexless night with the man, and he literally had me sprung. Just the thought of him made my heart skip a beat. When I was getting out of my car, my phone pinged several times. There was no doubt in my mind who it was. I unlocked the door to the apartment, sat on the living room sofa and dug in my purse for my phone.

The first message was a group text from Summer, "Go, Sis, I saw you sneak off with Terrance. Don't do anything I wouldn't do."

Aubrey responded, "Well, do everything I would cause I snuck away too, and I am about to put it on Landon's ass, lol."

I smiled.

The next message was from William.

It simply read, "Is it Friday yet?"

I texted back, "I wish!"

Still smiling while sitting on the sofa, I heard a noise. For the first time, I realized that I wasn't in the apartment alone. Instinctively, I hit 911 on my cell phone. I prepared my finger to hit the send button. I tiptoed towards the kitchen. The noise grew louder. When I reached the kitchen, I grabbed a butcher knife. I raised it above my head preparing for the stabbing position.

I jumped from behind the counter and yelled, "Get the…"

I couldn't believe what I saw. It was not a burglar or killer, but Aubrey and Landon's naked asses on the kitchen floor. He was giving her head. I scared the hell out of him. He yelled. Instead of Aubrey being scared, that heffa climaxed. She was shaking, moaning, and squirting. I couldn't believe my eyes. I had seen her naked countless times, but this was definitely something I hadn't ever seen or wanted to see. I dropped the knife on the floor and ran to my room. I felt completely embarrassed and taken aback. I lay down on my bed, unable to shake that image from my mind.

"Daaaammmmnnnn!" I yelled.

Aubrey knocked on my door, and yelled, "Sorry bestie!"

A few minutes later, I could hear their sexcapade continue in her bedroom.

Hearing their moans, groans, and grunts made me fantasize about William and me having sex. Sometime during my fantasy, I drifted off to sleep. I was awakened by Summer and Aubrey busting in my bedroom.

Summer said, "OMG, Riri, Aubrey just told me what happened. Please tell me you didn't catch Landon snacking between her legs on the kitchen floor?"

I said, "What!? What are you talking about?

Aubrey said, "Riri, wake your ass up! Tell Summer what happened. She don't believe me."

I sat up in bed, and they joined me.

Aubrey continued, "Y'all, Landon and I were dancing at the blood drive. With every move we made, we were turning each other on. After about three songs, we couldn't stand it any longer and decided to leave. Obviously, we got back to the apartment before Riri arrived. We were all over each other as soon as we walked through the door. We couldn't even make it to my bedroom. We didn't realize that you had come home, Riri That was until, all of a sudden, Miss Ninja Rambo appeared out of nowhere yelling with a butcher knife in her hand. When I looked at you, you seemed traumatized. The thought of someone watching me while Landon was eating me out excited me more, and I just exploded everywhere! Literally!"

Summer and I looked at each other and busted out laughing.

Aubrey said, "Y'all, I'm so serious; I have never climaxed that hard before in my life. That shit was the boom. Y'all should try it, too."

Summer said, "Aubrey, you are too much for me. But I may need to try it for real."

Again, we all laughed.

Summer turned to me and asked, "So where did you and Terrance go, and what did y'all do?"

I felt embarrassed and looked away.

Aubrey said, "Come on, Riri, don't hold back. Hell, you just saw me in my most vulnerable moment. So, spill it, Chicka."

I looked down at my hands and started fumbling with them, like Greyson.

Aubrey, gently touched my knee and said, "Is everything okay, Riri, did something happen? Did he hurt you?"

Summer put her hand on top of mine to prevent me from fumbling with them.

I said, "It's nothing, y'all. Everything is OK."

Summer said, "Are you sure, Riri?."

I said, "Look, nothing happened between Terrance and me. We are just friends and nothing more. After we left the dance floor, I thanked him for the dance, and we parted ways."

Both of them looked disappointed as if they wanted more. Honestly, I wanted to give them more, so I did.

I started, "Look, I have something I want to tell both of you, judgment free."

Summer said, "What do you mean by judgment free? We never judge each other. That's why we've been able to remain friends for so long."

I said, "Yeah, I know. But, what I'm about to say is a little embarrassing."

Both of them looked worried. I assured them that nothing bad had happened and that I just wanted to get some advice from them. I asked them to just let me say it without interruption or judgment.

They agreed, so I began.

"I met someone. It's someone I really like. I mean, he makes me happy. I know you two have one question in mind and it's, who? I can't tell you that right now. It's complicated and I would rather keep him a secret for now. Hopefully, things will work out between us, and I will get the courage to tell you who he is, one day. But, I don't know."

I paused for a few minutes to gain the strength I needed to continue.

"But, anyway, how do I say this? I need y'all to school me on some things; I want you to tell me what it is like. Tell me how you know for sure that he is the one."

They both looked at each other.

I laughed nervously and responded, "I don't mean it that way. We are not getting married or anything. I mean how do you really know whether or not he's the one that you want to give yourself to? I guess this entire conversation would make more sense to you if I'm totally honest with y'all. There's something that y'all probably don't know about me. I've never had sex before. I want to know what it is like, and if he's the one I should give myself to. Hell, I've waited this long, so I want to make sure I'm not making a mistake."

I stopped talking and looked at them. I expected them to respond but neither said anything.

After a few more seconds of silence, Summer asked, "Is it OK for us to speak now?"

I chuckled and said, "Whatever, heffa. Yes, it's OK to speak."

Aubrey took my hands and said, "Riri, first, there's one thing we both know about you. We know for sure that you have never had sex before, Miss Goody Two Shoes."

I pulled my pillow from behind me and hit her with it. We laughed.

"But seriously, Riri," Aubrey continued, "I can't explain how you know that he's the one. You just know it. He will be the one that will make your heart skip a beat. The one that you can't stop thinking about. On the other hand, Riri, honestly, sometimes it is just about sex, and some people are fine with that. Sometimes, a person wants a little more. From knowing you, I think that is exactly what you would want. Being that it will be your first time, you have to be careful because your first time can be an emotional time. So, please be careful. And don't be afraid to have your limits of what you are and aren't willing to do and accept. Most importantly, since you have waited this long, be sure he is the one you want to give yourself to."

Summer added, "Yeah, she's right, Riri. Be sure he's the one. If I could offer you any advice, I would say to make sure that the feelings are mutual. Because when they aren't, things can get really complicated. Feelings get hurt, and mostly, it ends up being the female who is hurting. So, just be sure.

I said, "I understand, I think. But what does it feel like?"

Aubrey said, "It feels good. Don't you remember what happened with Landon? Didn't you see my reaction?"

We laughed.

Then she added, "But seriously. It just depends. It can be uncomfortable, especially if it is your first time or if he's really big."

We laughed again.

She continued, "It can be awkward if neither of you know what you are doing. It can be disappointing if it's too quick, or he's all about him. It can be exhausting if it takes him too long to finish. But most importantly, it can be beautiful, especially if the feelings are mutual, and he's gentle and takes his time, and he makes sure you feel comfortable and safe."

Summer added, "When a man wants it to be more than just sex, he does more. He explores your body. He appreciates it. He cherishes it. He caresses it. He teaches you how to appreciate your body, and he appreciates it in return. It's a great feeling, Riri. But, like Aubrey said, make sure the feelings are mutual. Make sure he feels the same way you do. If not, it hurts later. It's the worst kind of hurt in the world, and that makes it harder to trust other men in your life. Also, it can make you feel desperate for love and attention, because you want the feelings to be mutual. We all know that we can't make someone love us."

I looked at Aubrey.

I said, "So tell me, which is it for you and Landon?"

Aubrey looked away.

She said, "Honestly, Cherry, this conversation makes me question so many decisions I've made in life. To answer the question you just asked, I would have to say that it's just sex. Landon is a good-looking guy and that's all I know about him. I've allowed my physical attraction to him get in the way of getting to know him. Like most women, I want to be a wife someday. I want to be wined and dined. I want a guy that makes me smile and is a good conversation piece. My mom taught me that those things depend on me. So, if I want more with Landon, then I have to slow things all the way down, if it's not already too late."

Aubrey started crying. Summer and I did too.

Through sobs I said, "Well, if it's too late, it's his loss, not yours."

We spent the rest of the night crying, laughing, and talking. Then, we fell asleep.

CHAPTER
SEVENTEEN

Hooked Me

The next few days dragged by. I thought Friday would never come. When it finally did, I was more nervous than ever. Dr. Nelson and I had talked every day up until Friday. He was out of town at another speaking engagement in California and was scheduled to arrive back in town later Friday evening. He told his wife that he wouldn't be back until Sunday so that we could spend the entire weekend together. The plan was for me to go our meeting spot whenever as soon as I got done with classes so that I would have time to shower, relax, and enjoy his place. He told me where to find the extra key. When I left my apartment Friday morning, I left with my spinnanight bag, filled with my necessities: lip gloss, whipped body butter, body oils, condoms, Sour Patch candy, Tic-Tacs, wipes, other overnight essentials. I let Summer and

Aubrey know that tonight may be "The Night" and that I would be back home on Sunday. We hugged, they gave me some last-minute advice, and we said our goodbyes.

When I finished my last class, I headed straight to Dr. Nelson's place; the ride seemed shorter. Once I pulled into the driveway, I smiled. The place seemed more beautiful than before. I stepped out of the car, opened the truck, and grabbed my bag. Then, I realized I was hungry, and I should have stopped to get something to eat before arriving. I decided I would find something in his fridge. I headed up the walkway, got the key from under the fake rock, walked up the steps, inserted the key into the lock, turned the knob, and stepped inside. I felt relieved once inside, grateful for not being seen.

Once inside, I was able to see the house with new eyes. It was something straight out of a magazine. It took my breath away. I explored the house for what seemed like the very first time. The house was decorated exquisitely. Gorgeous hardwood and beautiful area rugs adorned the floors. The walls were painted in warm colors. The ceilings were high; the draperies were custom-made. The kitchen had unique stone countertops, elegant faucets, and the most modern appliances. The bathroom had stone countertops with elegant sinks and faucets, natural stone floors, beveled mirrors, and floor to ceiling tile on one wall.

The master bedroom was a spacious retreat with high ceilings that created an open, airy atmosphere. Warm-toned hardwood floors extended throughout the room, adding a touch of elegance and natural charm. A grand king-size bed served as the focal point, featuring a plush headboard and luxurious bedding that invited relaxation. Opposite the bed, a stunning stone fireplace added a cozy element, its rugged texture contrasting beautifully with the smoothness of the floors. The large windows let in ample natural light, offering a panoramic view of the outdoors while bathing the room in a soft, welcoming glow during the day. A comfortable sitting area was tucked near the windows, complete with a pair of armchairs and a small coffee table—perfect for reading or enjoying a morning coffee. Mounted on the wall opposite the fireplace was a big-screen television, strategically placed for easy viewing from both the bed and the sitting area, making the master bedroom a perfect blend of comfort and style. To sum it all up, it was breathtaking, to say the least.

I placed my spinnanight bag by the bed and sat down to take it all in. I was startled by a familiar sound. At first, I wondered if it was in my head. I heard it again, just as clear as the first time. It was the doorbell! I jumped off the bed, hugged my purse, and searched for the quickest escape route. Who could be at the door? Did someone see me come inside, after all? Had I been set up? The police? His wife? No, she wouldn't ring the bell at her own home.

"OMG!" I breathed silently.

Fear got the best of me. I hid inside the closet. Once inside, I realized it had to be the first place a killer, or worse, an infuriating wife would look.

Suddenly, my cell started ringing. It scared the shit out of me and was enough to literally make me have a heart attack. I dumped everything out of my purse to get to it as quickly as possible, and I silenced it. I looked at the screen, it was Dr. Nelson.

"Damn!" I thought to myself, "He's calling me to warn me that my life is about to end." Barely making a sound, I answered the phone.

"Dr. Nelson!"

He said, "Cherry, why are you whispering? Is everything OK?"

I shot back quickly, "Hell no, everything isn't OK. As a matter of fact, somebody's ringing your doorbell, and I am hiding in the freaking closet."

He laughed.

I whispered in an angry tone, "Are you freaking kidding me? What the hell are you laughing at? What's going on, Dr. Nelson?"

At that point, he was laughing hysterically.

"Cherry, why are you hiding in the closet? There is no need for that. Sweetheart, please come out and answer the door."

"Are you insane?" I asked between clenched teeth. "There's no way I'm coming out of this closet to answer your freaking door."

He said, "Cherry, trust me. I will never do anything to intentionally hurt, harm, or set you up in any way. There's something at the door for you. Will you please answer the door?"

Although I was hesitant, I stood up. I slowly turned the closet doorknob, gently opened it, and peeked outside. My breathing quickened, and my heart raced even faster.

He said, "Cherry, you're a beautiful young woman. A beauty like yours is rare. It's hypnotizing. It's to be cherished. I cherished you, Cherry, and want to make you happy. Trust me."

Those words gave me a small sense of reassurance. I cautiously made my way to the front door and opened it. To my surprise, instead of the police, a killer, or his wife, I found myself facing a large arrangement of flowers. The delivery man asked me to sign for them. I closed the door and headed towards the kitchen. I placed the vase on the counter and reached for the attached card.

It read, "You are special and rare, just like these Middlemist Red Camellias. I will forever cherish our time together. Signed, William."

A wide smile spread across my face.

Dr. Nelson asked, "Is everything OK, Cherry? Are you still there? I apologize. I was just trying to surprise you."

I forgot he was still on the phone.

I smiled and said, "Dr. Nelson, everything's perfect. Thank you so much. I love surprises, especially this one."

He said, "I am so glad to know that about you, Miss O'Brien. You know, I am a man that can be full of surprises. I want you to take a warm bath. I placed a garment in the bathroom for you to slip on. I can't wait to see you tonight."

He hung up.

I thought to myself, "He just might be 'The One'!"

After my soothing, hot bath, my hunger returned with a vengeance—I felt absolutely famished. I headed into the kitchen to see what I could find in the fridge. It was fully stocked with all kinds of fruits, vegetables, meats, and beverages, but I wasn't in the mood to cook anything.

Then, it happened again. The doorbell rang and so did my cell phone. My heart started racing again. Of course, I went for my phone instead of the closet or front door. I put it to my ear without saying a word.

Dr. Nelson said, "Cherry, answer the door before your dinner gets cold."

I was speechless; it was like he could read my mind.

"How did you know?" I asked.

He laughed, then ended the call.

I was thankful for dinner: a farro salad, baked salmon, garlic-buttered asparagus, honey balsamic-glazed brussels sprouts, and roasted potatoes. I washed it all down with a glass of sweet tea. I was completely stuffed, and drowsiness quickly overtook me.

I must have drifted off while watching TV, because the next thing I knew, I felt a gentle kiss on my lips. I didn't need to open my eyes to recognize whose lips they were—his were unmistakably perfect. I parted my lips to welcome his tongue, warm and soft, filling me with a sweetness that took my breath away. My breathing quickened. With my eyes still closed, I sank back onto the sofa and pulled him on top of me, our rhythm unbroken. The kiss deepened with passion, and I craved more of him. When I finally came up for air, he continued, trailing kisses down my neck. His hands began to explore my body, untying the silk robe I wore, and he teased my sensitive nipples through the gown underneath with his tongue.

I felt like I was being touched for the first time. I did not realize how sensitive my breasts were until he started to suck and bite on them. It felt pleasurable and somewhat painful at the same time. My moaning told him how much I was enjoying it. He moved down lower. He kissed my navel. My "honeypot" was so wet; it was beating. I wanted him to taste me, but I was too embarrassed to ask. Instead, I spread my legs trying to inadvertently direct him to where I wanted him to go. He skipped right passed my spot and started kissing my inner thigh. I shifted my body slightly in an attempt to redirect him, again. Instead, he laughed that laugh I loved so much, then moved to the other thigh and started kissing it. This felt like pleasurable torture.

He moved on down my legs. I felt his warm, moist tongue slide between two of my toes, then he stopped.

He said, "Cherry, open your eyes. Let me see your eyes."

For the first time, I realized that I had not looked at him since his arrival. Slowly, I opened my eyes. The dim lights stung a little. When my eyes finally focused, I saw the most handsome face ever. Our eyes locked. He skillfully started licking my toes again. My body erupted with such intensity, and I let out a loud, uninhibited cry—not of fear or terror, but of pure pleasure. Dr. Nelson waited patiently for my breathing to steady before gently scooping me into his arms and carrying me to the bedroom. The rest of the night was simply... unforgettable.

When we entered the bedroom, Dr. Nelson gently laid me down on the bed. I have to admit, I felt a bit embarrassed by what had just happened in the living room. I had experienced that sensation before, but never with such intensity. It was as if Dr. Nelson had awakened every sense within me, and he didn't even need to lick me to do it.

After placing me on the bed, we locked eyes for a moment. He stepped into the bathroom and returned, the sound of running water filling the air. Taking his position at the foot of the bed, he removed his tie and unbuttoned his collared shirt. Our gazes never wavered. Next, he unbuckled his belt and pants and let them drop to the floor. My breathing quickened, yet our eyes remained locked on each other. Then, he slid onto the bed and gently pulled my gown over my head, revealing my erect nipples that seemed to crave his attention.

With both hands, he lifted my hips slightly and removed my thong, causing me to pant with desire. I longed for his touch, closing my eyes and spreading my legs in anticipation of his warm, moist tongue against my throbbing inner lips. But instead, he got off the bed, scooped me up into his strong arms once again, and carried me into the bathroom. He placed me next to the shower door, then reached down to remove his socks. Standing upright, he looked me in the eyes for approval before removing his boxers. I nodded, and for the first time, I saw his big, black, erect dick.

He crossed his arms, smiled the smile that I loved so much, and said, "Are you impressed?"

Impressed was an understatement, but I thought of something to say really quick.

"I'm just enjoying the scenery."

We burst into laughter.

"OK," he said, "Hopefully, things will get more enjoyable before the evening ends."

We laughed again, but deep down inside, I was scared as hell.

We stepped inside of his huge walk-in shower. Once inside, the water felt great to my body. But, my eyes were focused on his enormous erection.

He noticed me staring, and said, "It's real. You can touch it if you like."

I smiled. Too embarrassed to even touch it, I just stood in direct aim of the water. Dr. Nelson grabbed some body wash and squeezed it into his hands. He lathered it all over my body. His touch, alone, made my body shiver. He must have thought I was cold because he turned the dial to increase the temperature of the water. He used his hands to explore my entire body.

He started from my neck, then moved to my shoulders. He massaged my shoulders with his big, strong, soft hands. Then, he moved to my breasts. He cupped each one in each of his hands and caressed them. It felt good, yet sensual. I leaned my head back against his chest and moaned. His manhood was poking me. My nipples were hard. I never knew they could get that hard. Afterwards, he rubbed by waist, hips, butt, right leg, left leg, and both feet. He stood to allow the water to rinse the soap away.

Next, he licked and sucked my left breast. I moaned, and his licks and sucks became more aggressive. My nipples continued to stand at attention begging for more. He used both of his hands and cupped both of my ass cheeks without missing a beat with my left breast. He moved over to the right one and licked and sucked on it. He surely knew what he was doing. He skillfully gave it the same attention he had given the left. He then lowered himself to one knee. He lifted my left leg over his right shoulder and kissed my clit. I leaned forward to balance myself because my body was starting to shake. He used his tongue to lick all around the heart of my femininity. With Braylen, it was never this intense. Dr. Nelson's facial hair created an additional sensation that I loved. His tongue was warm and wet. He was licking and sucking my "honeypot" as if he had a degree in it. My body responded to every lick and suck he gave. My hips were grinding against his face. I was salivating. The shower water was tap-dancing on my breasts. The feeling was overwhelming. I tried not to scream. I tried to control my breathing. I tried to keep my balance. But Dr. Nelson was making it hard.

In between a lick and a suck, he said, "Cherry, cum for me!"

On demand, I exploded vigorously. I passed out, and he caught me in his strong arms. The next thing I knew, it was the wee hours of the morning.

I LOOKED AT DR. SARTORI AND SAID, "THE EXPERIENCE WAS EX-hilarating. He awakened something within me, making me feel alive, delicate, and special. He was patient, taking his time to explore and caress every part of me. With him, I felt like a breath of fresh air, as if it was safe to trust again. In those moments, all the pain I'd endured from Momma, Daddy, my brothers, and the Millers faded away. I was hooked."

Emotions overtook me.

I said, "Dr. Sartori, I think we need to take a break so I can gather myself and grab some lunch. Plus, I need to make a few phone calls."

She agreed and excused herself to the ladies' room, again.

CHAPTER
EIGHTEEN

Kissed Me

After twenty minutes, Dr. Sartori and I resumed our session. She looked drained and flushed, so I offered her a cup of coffee. She gladly accepted, and when I reached it to her, I think I felt her hand lightly but purposely brush against mine.

I was staring out the window, marveling at the busy streets of LA. Dr. Sartori took her seat and grabbed her pad and pen.

She said, "How did things end between you and Dr. Nelson?"

I turned around with a sly grin on my face and said, "Who said things ended between us?"

Her eyes widened. She said, "Are you implying that..."

I interrupted her and said, "Dr. Sartori, during this session with you, I will make no implications. I'm planning to share all details with you."

I reclined on the chaise lounge by the window. Dr. Sartori appeared uneasy, but I chose to disregard her discomfort.

I'M NOT SURE IF DR. NELSON WOKE UP BECAUSE HE SENSED ME moving or if he had been watching me sleep the whole time. When I opened my eyes, I found him staring directly into them.

He asked, "Hey, beautiful! How did you sleep?"

I asked, "What time is it? How long have I been asleep? Dr. Nelson. I didn't mean..."

He cut in, "Shhh, you have nothing to apologize for—except still calling me Dr. Nelson. That definitely has to change."

I interrupted, "But Dr. Nelson, I mean William, I was looking forward to us being together last night. I wanted it to be my first. I wanted it to be our first."

He interrupted again, "But we were together last night, and it was absolutely beautiful. Things went just the way I wanted them to go, Cherry. Last night was the best time I've had in a very long time. I want to remember and relive it for the rest of my life."

I said, "What do you mean? We didn't even do it. So, how was it beautiful?"

He interjected again, "Cherry, we don't have to have sex for things to be beautiful. You experienced something that took your breath away. I was a part of it and that's enough for me. Cherry, listen, you are new to this. We have no reason to rush things. We are going to make it memorable and beautiful. I plan to show you that sex isn't just about the physical."

I looked at him like he was crazy. He laughed.

He continued, "Sex is more mental and emotional, than physical. "It's about creating a deep connection between the mind, body, and soul. It's about bringing pleasure to your partner and truly understanding each other's bodies. It's about knowing precisely how, when, and where to touch. It's about being attuned to each other's physical needs. It's about speaking and listening to the body—and I have to admit, your body was speaking to me last night."

In a shy voice, I asked, "But what about you? Didn't you want to feel good too?"

He said, "Cherry, when you feel good, I feel good. Believe me when I say that last night was beautiful."

His words were so captivating that I found myself easily believing every one of them. I desired this man more than I had ever wanted anyone or anything in my life. I reached up and kissed him, and he responded with equal passion. My breath quickened as I pulled him on top of me. It was then that I realized that we were still completely naked.

I looked in his eyes and between breaths, I said, "William, show me."

William showed me. He kissed me. He licked me. He caressed me. He fondled me. He made love to me. The sex with him was quite uncomfortable. He was big, and I was small. Nothing of that magnitude had ever been inside of me. Let me correct that. Nothing had ever invaded my vagina other than a tampon and the metal thing the doctor used during a yearly exam When William tried to insert his dick into my "honeypot," it hurt. It was nothing like I had seen on TV, in the movies, what I had read about, or what Aubrey and Summer told me. It was a painful experience.

Every time he would try to inch his enormous dick inside, I would scoot up the bed. After a while, I had nowhere else to go but up the wall. He tried not to hurt me, and I appreciated his gentleness.

William was careful with me. He always checked to make sure he wasn't hurting me too bad and to make sure I hadn't changed my mind about continuing. Each time, I instructed him to continue. Honestly, that morning, he never got it ALL in. My "honeypot" had had enough. It hurt, burned, and felt like it had been split open. It couldn't take anymore. He knew because he didn't try to go any deeper.

During round two, he was able to go a little deeper. He began to grind against me. I was almost afraid to breathe. With every thrust upward, I would gasp. It hurt, but not enough for me to tell him to stop. He kept checking in on me, though. He kissed me, stroked my hair, and nibbled on my breasts. Then, he reached down and started massaging my clit. The sensation was incredible. I began to move against him, his moans filling the air around us.

He moaned, "Slow down, Cherry. You're going to make me cum. What are you doing to me?."

I replied, "The same thing you're doing to me."

We exploded.

He kissed me on the forehead and exited my "honeypot." It was relieved. I stayed wrapped in his arms, holding onto the moment, wanting it to last forever. I felt safe, loved, protected, and at ease.

Suddenly, I remembered something. I looked at him with fear.

I said, "I'm not on the pill. What should we do? I can't believe I didn't think to protect myself."

He pulled back the covers, exposing himself and the condom that he was wearing. He removed it, got out of bed, and headed for the bathroom. I smiled. Relief flooded through me. The last thing I needed was a baby, especially with a married man, or my professor. Hell, I don't know which sounded worse.

After a few minutes, he returned. Still naked, his manhood just as hard as it had been just a few minutes earlier. I moved closer to him, sensing he might be ready for another round, though I wasn't sure if I was.

Instead, that man, that warm, gentle, sexy ass man said, "I ran a warm bath for you. I want you to soak and relax—that was a lot, and I can imagine that it wasn't easy. Settle in and let the water soothe you... because I'm not finished with you yet!"

While soaking in the bathtub, Babyface's "Soon as I Get Home" echoed through the speakers in the wall. I checked my phone. Summer and Aubrey had texted a few times to make sure I was OK. I texted back to let them know that I was safe. I even told them that they would never believe what I just did. Of course, they sent back question marks.

Grandma had called around eight that morning, so I knew I needed to call her back. If not, she would start to worry, although I knew she had already called Summer and Aubrey's phone, too. If our parents could not get one of us, they would call all of us. I called Grandma.

She answered on the first ring. "Missy, where are you? Is everything OK? I called Summer and Aubrey, and they didn't answer either."

"Everything is fine, Grandma. I'm just taking a bath," I said.

Here I was again, lying to Grandma. I hated that. Technically I was taking a bath, so I guess I wasn't being totally dishonest.

"Hey, Grandma? How are you?" I asked.

"I'm fine. I just miss seeing and talking to my oldest granddaughter." she said.

I said, "Grandma, I miss you, too, but it hasn't been that long since we saw each other. I was just home."

She said, "I know, Missy. I miss having you home with me, that's all. The little time we do spent together makes me miss you even more."

"I understand, Grandma. I miss you too, and I love you more than you will ever know.

She asked, "Are you taking care of yourself, child? Do you need anything? Are you eating?"

"I'm fine, Grandma. I'm eating and I don't need anything. Between the money you and Greyson, Sterling, Momma and Daddy (and the Millers, I thought to myself) put in my account, I'm more than fine, Grandma, I love you and will call you back a little later."

She said, "Love you, too. God bless you, Missy. Let's pray before you go."

It didn't really feel right praying after what I had just finished doing and was planning to do again. But before I could interject, she began.

"Dear Heavenly Father, I lift up my granddaughter to You, asking for Your constant presence in her life. Be her guiding light, her pilot through all the journeys she undertakes. Help her to make wise choices, grounded in Your wisdom, and let her feel the profoundness of Your love, the greatest love of all.

Teach her the beauty of leaning on You, to trust in Your grace and mercy that sustain us daily.

Lord, grant her a servant's heart, one that seeks to honor and glorify You in all she does. Keep her safe, shielded from the evils of this world, and let her be a beacon of positivity and kindness to everyone she meets. Remind her to trust in You, to cast her cares and worries upon You, knowing You are her rock and refuge. Let her understand the importance of a deep and abiding relationship with You, for it is in You that we find our true purpose and strength.

I pray for guidance in her decision-making and ask for wisdom to help her choose her path carefully. Give her a heart that is open to Your word, sensitive to the whispers of the Holy Spirit, and willing to be led by You in all things. Use her to be a light to those around her, a testament to Your goodness, and a comfort to those in need.

I also bring before You the needs of her loved ones—her friends, family, and all who may be going through hardships. May they find peace, comfort, and hope in Your presence.

Thank You, Lord, for hearing this prayer. May her life reflect Your love, mercy, and grace. In Jesus' name, Amen."

She ended the call. A prayer that powerful definitely made me question the choices I just made. I truly felt convicted.

I stood, stepped out of the tub, and wrapped a towel around myself. I walked over to the vanity and looked in the mirror—I even looked convicted. Pulling the towel a bit tighter, I thought, "This must be what Adam and Eve felt when they disobeyed God and realized that they were naked in the Garden of Eden."

My hair was a mangled mess from getting it wet in the shower the night before. I reached for my spinnanight bag and grabbed by wide-tooth comb. I used it to detangle my hair and pulled it into a ponytail with a scrunchy. After that, I finished drying off. William was right. My "honeypot" definitely needed that soak. It was incredibly sore, and as I dried off, I noticed a small spot of blood on the towel.

I grabbed my whipped body butter and lathered it on. Then, I grabbed the silk gown hanging on the door. William was so thoughtful.

I was hit in the nose by the most enticing smell. It reminded me of home- the smell of a southern, home-cooked breakfast.

I stepped out of the bathroom, still feeling the sense of conviction lingering. William had prepared a spread of all my favorites: creamy cheese grits, sausage, crispy bacon, fried salmon patties, scrambled eggs with cheese, buttered toast with grape jelly, and freshly squeezed orange juice.

"Damn, how did he know?," I thought.

He smiled and said, "I hope you've worked up an appetite—I've prepared a feast fit for my queen."

I smiled and said, "Definitely!"

William pulled out my chair, then, took his own seat, reached for my hands, and blessed the food. As we shared breakfast, we talked about many things, but there was one question I was eager to ask.

After hesitating for a while, I finally asked, "What's really going on between you and your wife? She's never called when we're on the phone or when we're together. Are the two of you separated?"

He cleared his throat and said, "I figured this question would come up eventually. I want to be honest with you, Cherry, so here it goes. Lauren and I have been married for a long time. Like I mentioned before, we have a son, Landon, who's a student at Morehouse University. Like me, Lauren has a successful, demanding career—she's also an engineer. Her job requires a lot of travel, even more than mine. Right now, she's on one of her frequent business trips.

You actually remind me of her in many ways; you're both beautiful, intelligent, ambitious, and strong-minded. But Lauren has lost sight of what matters most—family. For years, she's prioritized her career above everything, including me, and it's really affected our marriage. We don't communicate the way we used to, and we only spend time together for Landon's sake. That's why she doesn't call; she's always busy. I don't even think she realizes she should or that married couples are supposed to stay connected. I used to call her often, but I stopped because she always seemed too busy. She's changed so much since we have been married, and she's no longer the woman I fell in love with. Work is her main focus now."

I interrupted, "So, is it me that you are interested in, or the woman your wife used to be- the wife you want her to be?"

He responded, "Cherry, don't misunderstand me. My feelings for you aren't related to my wife. While you both remind me of each other, she can't hold a candle to you. She doesn't possess the love and compassion I see in your eyes when I look into them. She doesn't share your appreciation for family, friendship, or sisterhood. Most importantly, she lacks the unique qualities that reside within you."

I replied, "But how can you be so sure I have that uniqueness? Looks can be deceiving. You don't really know me, William."

Tears began to stream down my face.

"There aren't many people I trust. I've been hurt by those who are closest to me, and it's difficult to move past that pain-pain that feels as fresh as it did years ago. I still carry it with me. William, I'm not the person you think I am. For instance, Summer and Aubrey are my best friends; they're like sisters to me. I've kept so much from them, yet they share everything with me."

I started to cry even harder.

"I can't even tell them where I am right now, even though I know they would share that with me if the roles were reversed. I know that they would never reveal anything about us or judge me for it."

William got up, came to my side of the table, knelt on the floor, looked in my eyes, and said, "Cherry, please don't think you have to keep anything from them. I trust you. If you trust them, you can tell them where you are and who you are with whenever you are ready."

He picked up the napkin from my lap and dried my tears and placed the warmest kiss on my lips.

William and I spent the rest of the day getting to know each other. I finally mentioned Daddy, Lisa, and Liv. He asked about my past boyfriends, and I told him there hadn't been any. Some secrets, as you know, are meant to be kept.

We moved to the living room, and watched my favorite movie, *Love and Basketball*. I loved how Quincy adored Monica; it felt like something out of a fairy tale. Plus, it made me incredibly horny. I got up from the couch and climbed on top of William, and we began to kiss. I can't remember if I mentioned it before, but William was an amazing kisser. It felt like he was making love to my mouth with his tongue—always warm and inviting, never too messy. I can't stand a sloppy kisser. He used his tongue to explore my entire mouth, knowing just when to tug on my bottom lip. That little pull was everything.

Since I wasn't wearing any underwear, the bulge in his boxers pressed against me in all the right ways, and I started to grind against it. William placed his hands on either side of my waist to match my rhythm. The friction of his manhood, through his boxers, rubbing against my clit was overwhelming. I reached down and pulled it out. There it was—big, chocolate, and standing proudly, waiting to be embraced. The veins running through it made it look strong and sinewy. I raised myself up and tried to lower myself onto it. "Tried" was an understatement. I couldn't even get the head in; it felt like my "honeypot" was being invaded. I grimaced and lifted my hips.

He said, "Take it slow, Cherry. Don't rush."

I didn't want to take it slow, so I tried again and again. It was just too painful. I gave up. At that moment, I was even more thankful for the warm bath from earlier.

I looked at it and asked it, "What are you? Where did you come from? You can't be real."

William grabbed my hand and said, "Cherry, you will get used to it because you'll have plenty of practice. Besides, it's probably a good thing that you weren't able to get it in because this time I'm not wearing a condom."

We shared a laugh as he got up from the sofa and guided me to the bedroom. He turned on the TV, so we could continue our movie. We laid together, falling in love like Quincy and Monica.

CHAPTER
NINETEEN

Chose Me

D r. Sartori, I feel the need to skip over some parts about William and me. Honestly, I can go on for days talking about our relationship: the dates, the romantic getaways, the wining and dining, the expensive gifts, and, of course, the sex. Let's just say this, things between us were magical, intense, astounding, mind-blowing. I finally got used to his dick, like he assured. I could take it anyway he dished it: missionary, cowgirl, cross, doggy style, lazy dog, woman on top, sitting on the throne, standing ovation, spooning, deep throat. You name it; I mastered it.

As far as Summer and Aubrey, they knew I was seeing someone, but I never told them who it was. They asked questions, but I could never bring myself to tell them it was Dr. Nelson. Deep down inside, I knew what William and I were doing was wrong, but I was in too deep and knew I wasn't going to stop. Besides, I just wasn't ready to part with their image of me being a "goodie-two-shoes"..

Based on what I've shared so far, one might think that William was the perfect man and wonder what more I could possibly want. And I would agree with that— he's perfect. I was head over heels for him, utterly in love. To be honest, I still love him to this day. He's truly amazing, but something changed between us. He introduced me to someone.

Earlier, I mentioned that there must be something about that junior year. Well, that's certainly true because, unfortunately for William, I ended up meeting his wife, and everything fell apart.

I remember it as if it were yesterday. William called me on a Wednesday morning and asked me to stop by his office around 5:00. I told him I would be there since my last class ended at 4:45.

He ended the call with, "Thank you, Miss O'Brien. I look forward to meeting with you."

I realized right away that it wasn't a personal invitation but rather a professional one. I felt terrified—too terrified. Was something wrong? Did anyone find out about us? Was he getting fired? Was I going to be expelled from school? Oh my God, what would Grandma think? Would my brothers go after William like they did Braylen?

I was a nervous wreck all day. As it got closer to 5:00, I felt myself getting sicker and sicker. I even left class at 4:30 because I needed time to collect myself. I went to the restroom to splash some water on my face, but once I got in there, my nerves took over, and I had to rush to the toilet to vomit. Things were about to get real.

As I was leaving, I remembered something Grandma used to say often: "When you make your bed, be prepared to lie in it."

Well, this was definitely a tough bed to lie in. I knew better than to get involved with a married man, especially one of my professors. What was I thinking? I loved William, but was it really worth it? It seemed I was about to face the consequences of my choices.

I took my time walking to his office, not wanting to seem too eager but also not wanting to show up late. At exactly 5:00, I gently knocked on his office door, hoping no one would answer, but I could hear voices inside. The only one I could recognize was his. I knocked again.

William opened the door and said, "Awww, Miss O'Brien, we were expecting you."

I looked at his eyes trying to get a clue as to what was going on, but I couldn't read them. I took a deep breath and stepped inside. A beautiful woman that I had seen pictures of was standing near the window, behind his desk, with her arms crossed. She was dressed in an off-white, two-piece suit with nude heels. Her hair was cut in layers with honey-brown highlights. Her skin was chocolate, the color of mine. Diamonds graced her ears and neckline. She had a pear-shaped diamond ring gracing her left ring finger. It had to be at least four carats. William took his place beside her. I felt myself getting sick again.

My hands started to sweat. My legs became wobbly. My heart started racing. My chest began to hurt, and I could feel myself overheating. My head starting spinning.

Spin

Spin

Spin

Spin

Spin

I looked at the both of them, wondering who would speak first.

Dr. Nelson spoke, "Have a seat, Miss O'Brien."

I obeyed, scared to disobey, but even more scared that I was about to die. William took a seat in his office chair. Instantly, I was reminded of the numerous times I had sucked his dick while he was sitting in that chair. My eyes fell to his desk. I was reminded of the countless times he had laid me on it to lick my "honeypot." Afterwards, my eyes shifted to one of the wingback chairs in the corner. I was reminded of the umpteen times I had buried my face in the seat of that chair so he could fuck me from behind.

"Damn," I whispered aloud but still under my breath.

William smirked. He must have been able to read my mind. He adjusted himself in his seat.

He started first.

"Miss O'Brien, I would like for you to meet someone, my wife, Dr. Lauren Nelson."

Then, it happened; I died, or for the moment, it at least felt like I did.

Mrs. Nelson uncrossed her arms, smiled, showing all thirty-two perfectly white teeth, and extended her right hand to me. I looked at her and at him. Why in the hell would this woman want the person who was fucking her husband to shake her hand? Was this an attempt for her to pull me in closer to stab me?

"I'm sorry," I said, while ignoring her hand, "I don't understand what's going on."

She said, "You're right, Will."

"Will, who in the fuck is Will?" I thought.

"She's just as beautiful as you said. If she has the brains to match, she's going to be perfect," she continued.

"I'm sorry. Can someone please tell me what's going on?" I demanded.

Withdrawing her unshaken hand, she said, "My apologies, Miss O'Brien, for the confusion. Will asking you to come to his office unexpectedly probably has you a little worried. Well, let me shed some light on the situation.

Like Will said, I'm his wife, Dr. Lauren Nelson, but everyone calls me Dr. L. I'm vice president of one of the largest engineering firms on the East Coast. I'm here to make you an offer that, hopefully, you won't refuse."

For the first time since stepping into his office, I think I stopped holding my breath.

She continued, "My firm has created an incredible opportunity for an aspiring engineer. We are looking for a young woman who obviously has the ability to take giant steps in this man's world of engineering. She will have the opportunity to complete an internship with our company. This would require, in addition to the commitment to this university, some traveling and other responsibilities. I'm looking for someone with outstanding technical, communication, interpersonal, problem-solving, and critical thinking skills. When I was discussing the doors which could open for a young minority in the field of engineering, Will said he couldn't think of anyone more deserving than you. So, I asked him to tell me more about you. He talked about you all night, so I knew I had to meet you. I made plans to be in the area today, so I asked him to see if you were available to meet with me. He contacted you, and here we are."

I nodded.

She added, "We have never offered an internship of this caliber, so I'm hoping this is one that you will consider."

"Wow!" I stammered. "Thank you so much—really, thank you both for this opportunity. What steps do I need to take? When do I get started?"

She continued, "Miss O'Brien, my husband is a man with a keen eye. He can usually spot an engineer a mile away. I trust his judgment. So, with that being said, you got the internship. I choose you. Or maybe I should say, we choose you. The internship is yours if you want it."

I couldn't believe what I was hearing.

I stood to my feet, flipped my hair behind my ear and said, "OMG, are you serious? Of course I want it. I would be honored to accept this opportunity."

Dr. Lauren Nelson smiled, showing those pearly whites, again, then re-extended her right hand. I gladly accepted it. As a matter of fact, when I finished shaking it, she grabbed her right shoulder. I looked at William. He was flashing his pearly whites, too. Hell, we all were.

After that, she told us that she needed to be excused so she could get back to work. She explained that she would be in touch soon with more details. As soon as she left his office, I screamed with excitement. I started talking so fast about how I couldn't wait to tell Grandma, Greyson, Sterling, Momma, Daddy, Lavender, Summer, and Aubrey. I watched as William turned toward the window, lost in thought. Curious, I stepped over to see what had caught his attention. It was Dr. Lauren, heading to her car. I glanced back at him; for a moment, he looked genuinely sad—really sad. For the first time, I saw something in him that unsettled me.

As soon as she drove off, I jumped the man. I was all over him. I pulled him away from the window and kissed him passionately. I unbuckled his belt, undid his fastener, and unzipped his zipper. I allowed his pants and boxers to fall to the floor. The "Chocolate Anaconda" was standing at attention. I dropped to my knees and grabbed it with both hands. Then I spit on it; he loved when I did that. I took it all in. Well, not all, because that was impossible. I took it in until it hit the back of my throat. He closed his eyes and began to wobble. I stopped, took it out of my mouth and massaged the head between my index finger and thumb.

I said, "William, keep your eyes open. Watch me. Don't close your eyes. If you do, I stop."

He took a deep breath, and I took it in, feeling it reach the back of my throat. I tightened my grip, moving in a steady rhythm, alternately releasing and tightening. His knees began to buckle—a clear sign his eyes were closed. So, once more, I paused.

He moaned, "Cherry, please don't stop. I can't keep my eyes open. It's too much!"

I said, "William, keep your eyes open. Watch me. Don't close your eyes. If you do, I stop."

He nodded.

I went back to work. The "Chocolate Anaconda" was oozing with pre-cum. I used my tongue to lick it all up, while moaning at the deliciousness of his nectar. I slide my tongue over its entire length, making sure to touch every inch of it. Next, I directed it towards the back of my throat. I felt like a pro. To imagine, just a few months ago, the thought of putting a man's penis inside my mouth disgusted me. I mean, it really took some convincing from Summer and Aubrey. They assured me, if those are the right words to use, that it was OK for me to put it in my mouth.

I reached down with the other hand and started massaging his balls. He loved when I did that. Finally, I released 'The Chocolate Anaconda.' Hell, I had to because my jaws were tired and needed a break. I focused on the head. I kissed it, licked it, and sucked it. I circled it with my tongue. He enjoyed every minute of it. I looked up at him. His eyes were closed, but I didn't care anymore. William reached down and grabbed my head. He pushed it down; his way of asking me to put it in my mouth again. I obliged. When I went back down on it, I couldn't control my gag reflexes. I came up. He pushed it back down. I still couldn't control my reflexes. I don't know if it was the sound of me gagging or my skills, but whichever it was, he exploded with fury. It was a mouth full. I hurried to his office bathroom to spit, because I hadn't quite mastered the art of swallowing.

CHAPTER
TWENTY

Pissed Me Off

Whative I told my family about the internship opportunity, they were ecstatic. Grandma wanted me to come to Texas for a congratulatory party. I told her that I was too busy with classes. I promised her that we would celebrate when I came home for Spring Break.

Summer and Aubrey, however, were a different story. We celebrated at a local club near campus, taking vodka shots all night. We danced, laughed, and honestly, it felt amazing to be with them. I'd been buried in studying for so long that I hadn't had much time for friends, and I definitely needed some girl time. Before we realized it, the club lights came on—it had been ages since we'd stayed out until closing.

On Saturday, as soon as I woke up, I reached for my phone on the nightstand, expecting to see messages and calls from William—but there were none. Instead, they were all from the other Nelson, Dr. Lauren. She'd asked me to call her as soon as possible, and her message sounded urgent. A sense of nervousness settled over me.

Damn, it was already after 2pm, and her messages started at 8am. Her last message was at 12:20.

"Shit," I thought to myself, "that's what I get for having too much of a good time last night."

I sat up in bed and re-dialed her direct line.

She answered on the first ring.

"Miss O'Brien, I'm glad you finally got around to returning my calls. My business partners are thrilled that you have agreed to accept the internship and would like for you to get started right away. In fact, we would like for you to come to our office on Monday as soon as your classes are over. Let's say around 5:00, so we can discuss the details of the internship. We look forward to seeing you on Monday. One more thing, Miss O'Brien, don't ever keep me waiting like this again."

Click!

The call ended abruptly, leaving me in shock. Suddenly, I broke down, crying uncontrollably. Summer and Aubrey rushed into my room and leapt onto my bed.

Summer said, "Riri, what's wrong? Did something happen to your grandma?"

I couldn't speak.

Aubrey added, "Please, Riri, tell us what's wrong!"

I tried so hard to tell them, but I couldn't get it out.

I said, between sobs, "Everyone is OK. I-I ruined my chances at the internship by going out last night. How could I have been soooo stu-stupid! My life is over. My career is over before it even started!"

Aubrey said, "But, Riri, that makes no sense. We did nothing wrong last night. We celebrated. We didn't break the law. We didn't bother anyone! What are you talking about?"

I said, "I don't want to talk about it right now. Please, just leave me alone so I can sort through this. I promise I'll explain and make more sense in a few."

"Ok, we'll be in the living room when you're ready to talk," Aubrey said.

As soon as they left, my phone rang—it was William. I declined the call. It rang again, and I declined it once more. Then came a text, followed by another, and another. Soon, my phone was constantly buzzing and ringing. After about an hour, I finally cried myself to sleep.

I was awakened by the doorbell. I pulled the covers over my head to drown out the sound. Summer and Aubrey knocked on my door. They did not wait for me to answer; they came in with pizza and a bottle of water.

Summer said, "Riri, it's after seven. You really need to try to eat something."

I said, "Summer, my life is over. I don't want anything to eat. I'll eat tomorrow when I wake up from this dream."

She placed the water and pizza on my nightstand, and they exited without a fight.

A few minutes later, I heard the doorbell, again. Seconds later, Summer and Aubrey burst through my door. They scared the hell out of me.

Summer demanded, "Riri, what in the hell is going on?"

I sat up in bed. Summer and Aubrey were looking scared too.

Aubrey said, "I'm serious, Riri. What's going on? You won't believe who's at the door asking for you!"

I stammered, "What do you mean? Who's at the door?"

Aubrey continued, "It's Dr. Nelson. He says he needs to speak to you regarding your internship with his wife."

I said, "What do you mean he's at the door?"

They did not have to answer the question, because standing in my bedroom doorway was Dr. Willam Nelson.

Our eyes locked. I was frozen. I did not know how to feel. He looked mad. No, he looked angry. No, he looked infuriated. Summer and Aubrey looked confused.

William's eyes were burning a hole through me. He was breathing so hard his nostrils were flaring. Summer and Aubrey looked at me for a sign. I didn't give one. They looked at him then at me again.

William spoke, "Miss O'Brien, it is very important that I speak to you, immediately!"

There was an emphasis on the word 'immediately.' He looked at Summer and Aubrey, expecting them to leave. They looked at me wondering if they should.

Through clenched teeth, I said, "Summer, Aubrey—I'm sure both of you know Dr. Nelson. Like I mentioned earlier, there's been an issue with my internship. But I can't imagine why Dr. Nelson would send her husband here instead of coming herself. Regardless, this is our apartment, and no one has the right to come in here suggesting you should leave."

I kept my eyes locked on his as I spoke.

I jumped out of bed, totally ignoring the fact that I was only wearing a cut off t-shirt and a pair of panties, opened my closet door, grabbed a pair of sweatpants and a hoodie, and slipped them on. I grabbed a tissue from the box on my dresser. I saw a glimpse of myself in the mirror. I looked a mess. My eyes were red and swollen from crying. I did not see that confident person Grandma raised me to be. Instead, I saw someone whose life was falling apart. Someone who was afraid of hurting the people she tried so hard to make proud. Just the thought of it scared me to death.

I walked to my bedroom door and said, "Summer and Aubrey, if you would excuse me for a minute, I'm going to step outside with Dr. Nelson. I won't be too long."

Summer looked at me uncertainly and asked, "Are you sure about this? Wouldn't it be safer to stay here with us while you talk to him?"

I turned to them and said, "I promise I'll be fine. I just need to talk to Dr. Nelson—to set a few things straight."

Besides, I said, trying to soften the mood, "If anything goes wrong, I know how to kick where it hurts."

I turned to William, and before I could stop myself, I said, "Let's go, William... I mean, Dr. Nelson." But it was too late—they'd already caught the "William" slip.

William followed me out of the door. We continued to walk in silence because I was pretty sure Summer and Aubrey's ears were tiptoeing behind us. We rounded the corner. I stopped, then realized it was too cold to have this conversation without a coat. I started walking again. He followed. I spotted my car but realized that I did not have my keys. I saw his car parked a few cars down, so I walked over to it. He used his fob to unlock it, opened the passenger door for me, then went around to the driver's door.

As soon as he closed the door, I shouted, "Who in the hell do you think you are showing up to my place like this? Have you lost your fucking mind?"

He said, "Cherry, are you serious? I've been worried sick about you ever since Lauren called me with some nonsense about you possibly not being the right pick after all for the internship. She said something about trying to call you all day, but you wouldn't return her calls. Then, Landon said something about seeing you and your friends at some party last night, and that really got her going. I started calling you and couldn't contact you either. I have been literally calling and texting you all day. After you wouldn't return any of my calls or texts, my mind went straight to the worse. I know how Lauren is when it comes to her career. That's all that truly matters to her. She did tell me that she finally spoke to you so I could only imagine what she said and how she said it. After you wouldn't answer my calls or texts, I couldn't help but feel responsible. After all, I am the one that introduced you to her. Cherry, look, I'm sorry for showing up at your place, but I felt desperate and didn't know what else to do."

He finally stopped talking. I looked at him. He looked at me. I saw hurt in his eyes, so much hurt that I started to tear up and almost felt sorry for him.

He grabbed my hand and spoke again, "Cherry, please say something, please."

I granted his request.

"Don't you ever show up at my fucking house again!"

With that, I got out of his car and slammed the door. I caught my reflection in his car window. That time, I did see the confidence Grandma instilled in me.

By the time I got back to the apartment, Summer and Aubrey were waiting at the door. "OMG, are you ok, Riri?" Summer asked.

"Yes, I'm fine. I'm just ready for this day to be over," I said, then I plopped down on the sofa.

"Tell us what the hell is going on," Aubrey demanded.

"Why did Dr. Nelson storm into our apartment that way? Or is it William now?" Summer questioned.

I sat down and started to explain, "Like I told y'all earlier, Dr. Lauren tried calling me all morning. I didn't answer because I was asleep. She left me several voice messages. When I finally called her back, she didn't really give me the opportunity to explain. She basically told me that I needed to be in her office Monday at 5:00 for an important meeting with her and her business partners. Then, she hung up. After that, she called Dr. Nelson and told him that he recommended the wrong person for the internship, so he tried calling me to ask me what happened, but by then, I had turned off my phone. When I stepped outside to speak with him, he explained that he knows how relentless his wife can be when it comes to her career. He assumed that she had fired me before I could even start working. He felt responsible and was trying to make sure I was OK."

Both of them looked at me like they weren't believing anything I was saying.

Summer said, "I hear what you're saying, Riri, but it still seems like things aren't adding up."

Aubrey spoke next, "Right! What are you not telling us? Why did you call him William, and it still makes no sense for him to come here?!"

I said, "I have no idea why he came here, but what I do know is, in my opinion, he was no longer Dr. Nelson once he stepped foot into our apartment."

The look they gave me told me that they still weren't believing me.

Summer said with an attitude, "Whatever, Riri. We aren't as stupid as you think we are. There is definitely more to this than you are telling us. Hell, for all we know he could be your mystery man or something."

I laughed a loud, fake laugh to cut the tension in the room.

Jokingly I said, "Hell, if he was my mystery man, I wouldn't still be living here with you hoes."

They both rolled their eyes. Summer even threw a pillow off the sofa at me.

I continued, "But for real y'all. Just that fast, I feel like my life is crumbling. It's like everything I've worked for could possibly be taken away from me because I missed Dr. Nelson's phone calls."

Aubrey said, "Look, Riri, you're right. Things may seem pretty bad right now, but you know what, who cares? If she takes this opportunity away from you, another one will come along. Don't allow anything or anyone to steal your joy. You have worked too hard. At the end of the day, you know that what's for you is for you and Dr. Lauren can't take that away. If this is not the internship for you, then there is another one out there that is. So, no more moping. Jump in the shower. Get dressed. We are going out to dinner so you can tell us the truth about you and William."

When she said "William" she stood up and did a raunchy dance.

I was about to protest.

Before I could, Summer said, "Riri, we will not take no for an answer. We will be leaving here in an hour."

Going out to dinner was just what I needed—I hadn't realized how hungry I was. It also took my mind off the internship. They did press me a bit more about William, but I stuck to my story, and eventually, they let it go.

On Sunday morning, we went to church. After everything I'd been through, I felt like I needed a little more Jesus. I went up for altar prayer, with Summer and Aubrey by my side. By the time we got home, I felt so much lighter. Grandma called, as she always did on Sundays, thrilled about the opportunities coming my way. Naturally, I didn't mention that I was upset. I didn't want to worry her. But, as always, she sensed something wasn't right in my voice, so she took it straight to Jesus in prayer.

"Father God, we come to you saying thanks, thanks for all you have done and all you will do. Father God, I ask for a special blessing for Missy. Whatever she is going through, I ask you to walk with her. Show her the way, Lord. I don't know what's going on with her right now, Lord, but I know that You do. The enemy is riding her back. He's trying to kill, steal, and destroy her. So, God, I need You to intervene on her behalf. I need You to help her to understand that the enemy wouldn't be coming against her if he didn't know that You had a plan for her life. Help her to understand that the enemy can be taken down with Your words alone. This is not her battle. The battle belongs to You, Lord. Forgive her Lord. Forgive her for all the wrong she has done. Forgive her for all the days she has forgotten to come to You during the good times and the bad times. Forgive her for all the days she hasn't given thanks."

She paused for a moment, then continued.

"Father, I ask you to fill her with the power of Your holy spirit. Fill her with Your discernment and wisdom. Teach her that the power of life and death is in the tongue. Teach her that she can ask, and it will be granted. Lord, I thank You for the constant reminder that Your presence is always with her. I thank You, God, that no weapon formed against her shall prosper. May You bless her and keep her. May You turn Your face towards her and be gracious towards her. I pray that You will give her all that her heart's desires and everything she needs pertaining to holiness and grace. These and other blessings I ask in Your son Jesus's name, Amen.

P.S. God, remind Missy that she has survived too many storms to be bothered by raindrops."

Of course, by the end of that prayer, the tears were flowing. Grandma sure knew how to make a girl feel guilty of sin.

CHAPTER
TWENTY-ONE

Filled Me Up

William tried calling me repeatedly on Sunday, but I did not have time for his mess. I was still angry at him for showing up at my place. I mean, the nerve of him.

By Monday morning, I was ready for anything. Classes flew by. With my last class ending at 2:30, I had plenty of time to go home, shower, and change before heading to my first day at the new internship. I wore an Alexander McQueen single-breasted lace peplum blazer with a lace-back wool-blend pencil skirt and Tom Ford black leather with gold spiked heels. With the steady flow of money from my family Williams, and the Millers, I could afford things most of my peers couldn't. I needed this internship and wanted it badly, and I was dressed like I'd already earned it—which, technically, I had.

My hair was styled perfectly, flowing past my shoulders, and my chocolate skin was flawless, requiring little makeup. I looked like a million bucks, with the walk, confidence, and attitude to match. When I arrived at the engineering firm, I checked in with the receptionist, who notified the team and led me to the waiting area. I didn't wait long before Dr. Lauren entered. I stood to greet her, and although she tried to hide it, I could tell my appearance caught her off guard—just the reaction I'd expected.

She cleared her throat and said, "Good to see you this evening, Miss O'Brien. Follow me into our conference room."

I followed Dr. Nelson to the elevator. We rode up in silence, but I felt a little uncomfortable because she kept looking at me. We stepped off, and she cleared her throat again.

"My partners and I are excited about this opportunity for you. I think I'm more excited than they are. I don't have to tell you that there are not a lot of women in this line of business, especially at this level. This way, Miss O'Brien."

She opened the door to an enormous office, and I stepped inside. I had not been fully prepared for what I saw. Although I knew engineering was often considered a "man's world," the scene before me made it strikingly clear. The room was expansive, with windows lining three walls and a massive flat-screen projector covering the fourth. A large conference table sat in the center, surrounded by leather chairs, all but two of which were occupied.

Each person stood as we entered, and none looked like Dr. Lauren or me. They were all White men—at least twenty of them. In my mind, I could almost hear James Brown's voice singing, reminding me, 'It's a man's world.' I straightened my peplum jacket as James Brown continue to sing in my head.

As Dr. Nelson showed me to my seat, the men in the room eyed me from head to toe. After introductions, they got right to business, discussing topics like company economics, performance metrics, competitor analysis, industry updates, department news, new projects, partnerships, technological advancements, testing strategies, and more. They even connected with various local, state, and international partners, displaying countless charts and graphs on the screen. Much of the information was unfamiliar to me, but I took plenty of notes. Finally, at around 10:15 p.m., the meeting concluded.

Dr. Nelson and I stayed behind to go over the details of my internship contract, including my stipend, schedule, roles, and responsibilities. By the time we finished, it was well after midnight. We exited the building together, and neither of us mentioned the missed calls from Saturday morning.

When my alarm went off Tuesday morning, it felt like I'd just gone to bed. I was exhausted but still energized from the meeting. Once again, classes flew by, and I was excited to get to work. Dr. Nelson spent a lot of time going over details of their high-end clients and shared her agenda for an upcoming West Coast project later in the week. She outlined the project's specifics and what I needed to do to help her prepare. The rest of my week was busy, so I felt a bit of relief when Friday finally arrived. With Dr. Nelson leaving town, I could finally rest and relax. I'd been so focused on work that I barely had time for anything else. Before she left, she advised me to get some rest because the next week would be intense, which almost made me choke—I wondered how much busier things could get!

The first thing I did when I got home was call Grandma. I hadn't really had a chance to talk to her, and I immediately picked up on the sadness in her voice; I knew it was simply because she missed me. I reassured her that Spring Break was just a few weeks away, and we'd spend some quality time together. That seemed to lift her spirits a bit, but I still felt bad knowing she was lonely. After our conversation, I took a shower, then headed to the fridge, starving. I could tell I'd lost a few pounds—balancing school and late hours at work had left me with little time to eat. I found some homemade pasta, spooned it into a bowl, and popped it in the microwave. While it warmed, I grabbed the remote and turned on the TV.

The doorbell rang—it was another delivery. They'd been arriving all week. Ever since our heated argument the previous Saturday, William had been sending me gifts. Although I still wasn't taking his calls, he hadn't stopped trying. On Monday– flowers and a spa tower. On Tuesday– a chocolate treasure box filled with gourmet cookies and brownies. On Wednesday– an organic gift box with handmade soaps, natural lip balm, organic tea bags, raw honey sticks, and more. On Thursday– e gift cards from some of my favorite stores.

I tipped the delivery guy, placed the gift on the counter, and checked on my pasta in the microwave. It wasn't quite ready, so I added more time to it. The delivery caught my attention again, but I wasn't quite ready to open it. I missed William so much, but I was still mad at him for showing up the way he did. He could have ruined everything. I mean everything. At the same time, I understood why he was worried about me and all. I got my food out of the microwave, sat on the sofa, picked up my phone, and decided to call him.

He answered on the first ring.

He didn't say anything and neither did I. I could hear him breathing.

I said, "Are you there?"

He said, "I'm here, Cherry. I'm afraid to speak; afraid that I may say the wrong thing, and afraid that you may hang up. I would rather listen to you breathe. Just knowing you are there on the other line is enough for me."

I said, "William, I was so angry with you. I'm still angry with you. Do you know what could have happened by showing up at my place? You should have known better."

He said nothing.

I continued, "This week has been exhausting for me. I have missed you so much. I'm caught between being angry, busy, missing you, and feeling lonely. Thanks for the gifts. I've been receiving them all week. I haven't had the opportunity to enjoy any of them because of work and school. Wish I could say the same for Summer and Aubrey, though. They have been eating all the stuff you've sent. I told them that they will definitely gain all the weight I've lost this week due to my lack of eating."

He interrupted, "What do you mean by lack of eating? Why aren't you eating?"

I said, "Because I've been too busy to eat. Your wife is a demanding lady, William. But I don't have to remind you of that. She keeps me just as busy as she is, so busy that I find myself skipping meals and not having much time to do anything else. I called Grandma today, and I could hear the sadness in her voice from not talking to her this week like we usually do.

William interrupted me, "Cherry, my wife's career is her life. You and I know that there is more to life than work. Family is important. Friends are important. Love is important. Don't ever let anything come between those things."

He sounded so serious when he said that, but I rolled my eyes and said, "William, I know that. That's why I promised Grandma that I'm coming home for Spring Break and that we would spend time getting caught up."

Then he asked, "What about us, Cherry? Can we spend some time getting caught up, too? I know that me saying I'm sorry is not enough, so let me prove it to you."

It didn't take much convincing for me because I missed him too, so I said, "When and where?"

His response was simple. "I'll see you at our place in an hour."

I hopped off the sofa and ran back into the kitchen. Without eating, I put my bowl in the sink. I noticed the delivery, again. I decided to open it. It wasn't chocolates or brownies or lavender or gift cards. It was a beautiful, diamond tennis bracelet with matching diamond-studded earrings. There was only one word to describe them: blinding!

I LOOKED UP AT DR. SARTORI FOR A MINUTE AND SAID, "AT THIS point you probably expect me to tell you about a wild sex-capade that William and I had when I arrived at the house, because that is exactly what I expected when I got there. As a matter of fact, that's what I wanted, but it was the complete opposite. William was a total gentleman. He spent the entire weekend showing me how sorry he was. Once I arrived, we traveled a few more hours to a ski resort. Going out in public together wasn't something we did too often. We shopped, dined, skied, went sightseeing, got a couples massage, and went to a live theater show. Of course, sex was a part of it, but not the most important part. That's what made it so easy to love William. He connected with me mentally, emotionally, socially, and of course, physically. Our drive back home was full of conversation and laughter. In the words of James Foxx, "when I first saw you…"

When we turned onto William's street, my heart skipped a beat. I sat up straight in my seat. I put my right hand on my chest and my left hand on his thigh. I could not speak. He started to slow down but not slow enough for me. He stopped before turning into his driveway.

I said, "OMG, where is my damn car? It's gone!"

He said nothing. He just smiled, then turned into the driveway and put the car in park. He opened his car door and got out. I sat frozen. He came around to my side of the car and opened my door. I remained seated. He reached for my hand. I couldn't move.

He said, "Cherry, get out of the car. How many times do I have to assure you that I won't let anything happen to you?"

I extended my right hand. He took it, and hesitantly, I got out of the car.

I said, "Where's my car? Do you think your wife's here?"

He answered, "Cherry, Lauren is not here. She is not due back in town until later tonight. You should know that; you planned her itinerary. To answer your other question, your car is right here."

Parked in his driveway was a brand new polar white Mercedes Benz.

I questioned, "What do you mean?"

He said, "This is your car, Cherry O'Brien. I bought it for you!"

I questioned, "Why would you do that?"

He answered, "Because you deserve it, and I wanted to."

I said, "William, this is too much. I can't accept this."

He asked, "Why not?"

I said, "I just can't accept it."

He said, "Well, you have no choice. It's paid in full. The title is already in the mail. It is your congratulatory gift for earning that huge internship."

I interrupted, "But I didn't earn it. I got it because of you."

He said, "Cherry, you got it because you are smart and ambitious and a go-getter. You did earn it and don't you ever think any differently."

I said, "William, I could never explain how I can afford a car like this. Really, this is too much. Plus, how can you explain a gift like this to your wife?".

He said, "Cherry, you don't have to worry about Lauren. Like I said before, our relationship has been rocky for a long time. So, for the most part, our finances are completely separate."

I almost hated I asked that question because he started looking sad.

Then he asked, "Are we going to just talk about the car, or are you going to take me for a ride?"

I couldn't help but smile.

I got in the driver's seat. The interior was classic red and black leather, trimmed in black, piano lacquer with flowing lines.

He hopped in on the passenger side. We took a couple of laps around the block, but only a couple because I couldn't wait to get back to the house to show him how much I loved and appreciated him and his gift.

When I left William's place, I called Summer and Aubrey and told them that I had a surprise for them. They made a joke about it being food because of all the goodies I had received during the week. When I got home, I called them again and asked them to meet me in the parking lot. They couldn't believe their eyes. They ran to the car. They were too excited. Of course, I had to kinda, sorta lie and tell them that that the car came with the internship. Ok, so I totally lied to them.

I went to sleep that night on cloud nine with Jamie Foxx singing in my ears "That's My Dream."

BY THE END OF MARCH, THE INTERN WAS GOING WELL, AND I HAD pretty much established a routine: class, work, class, work, class, work. I was able to squeeze William in on the phone, and occasionally on weekends. Dr. Lauren and I had a pretty good working relationship. I had to give it to her; the lady knew her stuff. When she walked into a room, she demanded respect, and it was given to her. She was an engineering guru and was training me to follow in her footsteps. During my time with her, she ensured that I had a balance of theoretical knowledge and practical experiences. Many of her colleagues and business partners knew me by name because of her. It was like she and I were becoming attached at the hip. We often spent our evenings eating dinner while discussing manufacturing, product and process development, IT support, consultancy, data management, research and development, logistics, sales, and management and administration.

CHAPTER
TWENTY-TWO

Tasted Me

S uddenly, things took a turn. Dr. Lauren and I were in her office, having dinner and going over the five-day lecture she was preparing. We were putting the final touches on her presentation when my phone rang—it was Grandma. I stepped out of the room to take the call, and when I returned, I was overjoyed. I excitedly shared my plans for next week, Spring Break, and the time I'd be spending with Grandma.

I said, "The closer it gets to Spring Break, the more excited I become." Without batting an eye, the bitch looked at me and said, "Sounds like a lot of fun, Miss O'Brien. I hope your grandma isn't too disappointed when she finds that you will have to change your plans."

I asked, "Change? Huh? What do you mean?"

She continued typing on her laptop and with a Grinch-like smile said, "I forgot to tell you that I need you to attend this business meeting with me. Five days is a long time to not have my right-hand woman with me, especially on a trip with this much at stake!"

I chuckled. Because I assumed she was joking.

For the first time, she stopped what she was doing and looked at me.

She said, "Did I say something funny?"

I said, still chuckling, "I thought I heard you say that I was going to California with you."

She said, "Well, I'm glad you find this amusing—I was worried you'd be upset. It seems you're handling the news better than I expected."

I jumped out of my chair and shouted, "Are you serious right now? There's no way I'm missing Spring Break with my grandma! We've been looking forward to this time together, and I'm not about to let her down."

She started back typing and in a calm voice said, "Miss O'Brien, I see we have a problem. You need to decide what is more important to you: this internship, which is a once in a lifetime opportunity, or your spring break, which comes around every year just like all other holidays, vacations, birthdays, and other foolish things. So, like I said in the beginning, I hope your grandma won't be too disappointed when she finds out that your plans have changed."

My eyes began to sting as tears started streaming down my face. I tried to hold them back, but I couldn't. I quickly shoved my papers into my briefcase, threw everything else into my purse, and rushed out the door. I hurried to the elevator, repeatedly pressing the down button. Once inside, I collapsed to my knees with tears. When I reached the first floor, I ran to my car as fast as I could. I called William, and when he answered, I just cried into the phone. He let me, without saying a word.

After a few minutes, he said, "What did she do, Riri?"

I told him how ridiculous she was; how she said those awful things to me with that evil smile on her face, without feeling, or compassion.

He said as gently and as compassionately as he could, "Cherry, you don't have to go. You have the right to say no. Other opportunities will present themselves. Your grandma is more important. Family is more important. Bottom line, tell her you aren't going, even if it costs you this internship."

Through sobs, I said, "William, I can't tell her that, and you know I can't. This is so unfair."

He agreed, "You are right, Cherry. This isn't fair. It's not fair that I put you in this situation. I knew how my wife was before I suggested you. Nothing is more important than her career. I shouldn't have put you in this position. I am sorry, Cherry. This is all my fault. I will speak to Lauren about this immediately."

I said, "William, you can't do that. You can't say anything to her. Please don't."

He said, "I have to. It's not fair to you. I can't let her get away with this."

I said, "William, please don't say anything to your wife. Let me handle this."

I heard something shatter right before he yelled, "Dammit, Cherry!"

I said, "William, I'll call you back. I need to call Grandma."

Grandma was hurt, to say the least, though she did her best to hide it. She tried to find the right words to comfort me, but it didn't ease my guilt. I couldn't bear the thought of letting her down. She reassured me that she understood and reminded me that my hard work would pay off in the end.

WHEN THE CAR ARRIVED TO TAKE US TO THE AIRPORT, WE RODE in silence. I had nothing to say. I put on my headphones to make it clear that I didn't want to talk. The flight from the East Coast to the West Coast felt long and lonely. I missed my family and friends and started questioning my decision. Maybe I should've taken William's advice, but it was too late, now.

When we checked into the hotel, I was surprised to find we'd be sharing the same suite—or rather, apartment, considering its size. Still, I didn't want to be anywhere near her. She explained that having a shared suite was necessary so we could keep working during our "downtime." William was right; she didn't know when or how to stop.

I spent Sunday avoiding Dr. Lauren as much as I possibly could, which wasn't much because all she wanted to do was talk about the upcoming lecture. When we weren't together, I was either on the phone with Grandma apologizing to her over and over again or with William telling him how much I hated his wife. By the time we finally got to bed Sunday night, Dr. Lauren and I were more than ready for Day 1 of her presentation.

Day 1: It was a breeze. We covered introductions, expectations, and objectives for the week. Honestly, I couldn't see why she needed me there, and I made sure my body language and expressions made that clear on the ride back to the hotel.

The rest of the evening was spent reviewing the agenda for Day 2 and adding final touches—again, she didn't really need me for any of it. I ordered room service and tried to enjoy it alone in my room.

Day 2: Things got intense. I have to admit, she impressed me; her brilliance was undeniable, and she reminded me why she was a damn genius. When we finally returned to the hotel, I was still mad at her, but probably a little less. She ordered room service before I had the chance, so I ended up eating with her in the dining area. She'd changed out of her business suit into shorts and a T-shirt, and I did the same. With her hair pulled back in a low bun, and no makeup, she looked surprisingly normal. Her skin was flawless, and I could see why William had been attracted to her. She turned on the TV, skipped the briefcase and laptop for once, and somehow, we ended up watching an entire movie together. I can't even remember what it was, but we laughed and ordered dessert, too. That night, work didn't come up at all. "Maybe she could actually be cool if she weren't such a bitch," I thought.

Day 3: Things were just as engaging as Day 2. When the session ended, I expected the driver to head straight back to the hotel, but when I looked out the window, we were on Rodeo Drive.

She put her hand on my knee and said, "Miss O'Brien, you didn't think we would come all the way to California and not go shopping, did you?"

The car stopped, and we stepped out—and let me tell you, we shopped. It had been ages since I'd shopped like that. Actually, I'd never shopped like that before. Dr. Lauren insisted we attend the rest of the conference dressed in only the finest, so everything we bought came from upscale stores and exclusive boutiques. The best part? It was all charged to the company's credit card. Back at the hotel, we had dinner and watched another movie.

Around 1:00 a.m., a severe storm rolled through, knocking out the power. Eventually, the generator kicked in, but the thunder was loud, and lightning lit up the sky. I was terrified. Finally, I got out of bed and looked out into the suite's sitting area, where I saw Dr. Lauren. I decided to step out of my room.

She asked, "Are you OK, Cherry?"

That caught me a little off guard because I had never heard her call me Cherry before.

I said, "Yeah, I'm fine. I just don't like thunderstorms."

She said, "I don't either, especially these kinds. I'm hoping it will pass soon."

"Me too," I agree.

"You're welcome to sit with me if you want to. I'll fix you a cup of warm tea," she said.

She didn't have to ask me twice. If I were back in Georgia, Summer, Aubrey, and I would be huddled up in the same room until the storm passed. After about an hour, it finally calmed, and we went back to our separate bedrooms.

Unable to sleep, I called William. I told him about the shopping spree, dinner, movie, the storm, and the surprising change in his wife. He was shocked, to say the least. We didn't talk long; I could tell he was tired, though he tried not to show it. A few minutes later, I heard a soft knock on my bedroom door.

"Yes?"

Dr. Lauren asked, "Cherry, can I come in for a minute?"

I answered, "Sure."

She sat at the foot of the bed. She said, "Cherry, I need to talk to you about two things. First, I'm sorry."

I interrupted, "Sorry?"

She continued, "Please, let me finish. Sorry isn't something I say too often. I'm sorry for not allowing you to visit your grandma. I can tell that family is important to you, and I shouldn't have gotten in the way of that. I remember a time when family was important to me, too, but I allowed work to get in the way of that. So, yes, I'm sorry."

She paused for a moment. I could tell she had more to say, so I didn't speak.

"I've noticed that you talk to your grandma every day, several times a day. I can tell that you miss her and that she misses you too. I can tell that you love her and that she loves you. I was wrong, I'm truly sorry. I wish I had that. I wish I missed someone like that and that someone missed me. I haven't spoken to my son or husband since I've been in California, and that's all my fault. When I first started going on business trips, they would call me all the time, but I never had time for them. After a while, the calls became less and less until they eventually stopped. Seeing and hearing you talk to your grandma made me realize how much I miss that. It makes me wish I could get that back."

I'm not sure when it happened, but I started to cry. I was crying because I missed Grandma, because my anger toward Dr. Lauren had resurfaced, because I felt pity for her, and because, once again, I was overwhelmed with guilt over my affair with her husband.

Dr. Lauren went into the bathroom. She came back with Kleenex. She sat on the bed next to me and gently dried my tears, but they didn't stop. She leaned in closer and allowed me to lean my head on her shoulder. After a few minutes, I calmed down. I started to feel better. I felt consoled. She rubbed my right shoulder with her right hand. The strap of my gown fell off my shoulder. I expected her to fix it, but she didn't. Instead, she pushed it further down and continued rubbing my arm. She placed a delicate kiss on my forehead. At first, I thought it was a kiss of comfort. You know, one that a mother gives a crying child, but something felt different about it; it felt sensual. Then, she lifted my chin and kissed me on the lips.

I said, "Dr. Lauren, what are you doing? Are you OK?"

I didn't know what else to say or ask. I didn't know if I was making more of it then I should have or if she was still acting as a mother consoling a crying child.

Dr. Lauren said, "Cherry, I have wanted you from the very first day my husband introduced us. I have tried to fight this feeling."

She said this while placing small kisses on my neck.

I said, "Dr. Lauren, I think you're mistaken. It's late. We both need some sleep. You're my boss, and you're a woman, and I am sorry if I've misled you in any way."

She said, "Oh, Cherry, I'm not mistaken at all. I know you are a woman, a beautiful woman, a woman I can't get off my mind."

She pushed the other strap off my shoulder revealing both of my breasts. Both of us looked down at them. Without hesitation, she positioned herself in front of me and began sucking on my left one.

I wanted to protest. I wanted to stop her. I really did. Part of me was scared. Part of me was shocked. Part of me was confused. Part of me liked it.

My breathing increased. Finally, I said, through heavy breaths, "Dr. Lauren, what are you doing?"

She didn't answer.

Instead, she kissed my lips. I think I kissed her back. She gently pushed me back on the bed and eased on top of me. She stopped and looked at me. I felt embarrassed. I think she sensed it because she smiled. She started sucking on my right breast. My gown started rising. I tried to push it back down. I eased up the bed. She eased up with me. Then, she reached under. I wasn't wearing any panties. She used her fingers and started massaging my clit. That's when I realized my "honeypot" was wet. My mind started spinning.

Spin

Spin

Spin

Spin

Spin

Spin

She started rubbing it faster. She stopped, locked eyes with mine, and slid her fingers in her mouth.

She said, "Cherry, you taste so good. Do you want me to stop?"

I didn't answer, she started fondling my "honeypot" again. It felt so erotic. My senses were awakened.

She said, "If you want me to stop, just tell me."

I don't know where it came from or why I said it, but instead of saying stop, like I was thinking, I said, "Don't stop now, Dr. Lauren. Taste me!"

She did for the rest of the night. We got no sleep. She made cum time after time after time. She tasted every inch of my body. She knew how to touch me. She knew where to touch me. She knew my body. It was as if it was made for her.

It felt like a dream, but I knew it wasn't because, like I said, we never slept. When she was done with me, she got out of bed without saying a word and closed my bedroom door. I laid in silence, stunned at what just happened. So many thoughts were running through my mind. "Did I really just have sex with a woman?" was the first question that popped in my head. "Did I really just have sex with the wife of the man I'm in love with?" was the second question. I don't know which question bothered me more. I pulled myself out of bed and jumped into the shower. I let the hot water wash away all traces of her. When I got out of the shower, I went through my normal morning routine and quickly got dressed. I sat on the bed; too embarrassed to step out of the room, too embarrassed to face her. I knew I had to muster up the courage. When I opened the door, she was sitting at the table drinking a cup of coffee and looking at some papers. She didn't say anything at first. Neither did I. Finally, she spoke.

"Cherry, I hope you don't mind me calling you that, you look stunning this morning. I fixed you a cup of coffee. About last night, I totally lost control. I couldn't help it. I won't apologize for what happened unless you want me to because I'm not sorry and will do it again when given the chance. I enjoyed every minute of it. When we started talking earlier, I told you that there were two things I wanted to tell you. The first thing was about your grandma, which I think I covered pretty well. I never got to the second thing. Before I get to that, I want to talk to you about something else." I waited for what would come next.

"I must be honest with you about something. Cherry, like I told you last night, I've wanted you since the day my husband introduced me to you. I've tried fighting these feelings ever since. I've tried being mean to you. I've tried not being around you as much. I've even considered firing you, all in hopes that these feelings would go away. But they haven't, actually, they intensified."

She grabbed my hand.

She continued, "Years ago when I was in college, I dated a woman. She was the love of my life. She was beautiful, kind, and gentle. You remind me so much of her. I was too ashamed to be with her, too ashamed of what my family might say. We had been dating a while I met William, and we started dating. He was everything I could ever want in a man, but he was not her. In addition, he was what my family wanted for me, so I pushed her away. Eventually, she stopped pursuing me, but I never stopped loving her. I never forgot about her. You showed up, and instantly I fell in love all over again. I was reminded of what I could have had with her. You are beautiful. You are ambitious. You are bold. You are courageous. It's like I've known you all my life, even though I've just met you. I've never met someone like her until William introduced us. Last night was perfect. It was magical. I hope that I get to enjoy it many times over."

She took a long pause.

Then she continued, "Now, I need you to hurry and get downstairs, or you're going to be late. You have a plane to catch."

Confused, I glared at her until she clarified what she meant.

She said, "Cherry, that's the second thing I wanted to talk to you about. You are flying back home. There's a car waiting to take you to the airport. Hurry before you miss your flight.

I didn't know what to say. I didn't know whether to thank her for allowing me to go home or to hate her for totally turning me out. Nevertheless, I didn't have time to decide which one. I jumped up from the table, ran to my room, and started stuffing things into my suitcase.

She came in and said, "Cherry, leave that. I've made sure that you have everything you need for your stay once you get to Texas. Besides, none of this stuff will work anyway. It's dresses, suits, and heels. I don't think you and your grandma will go anywhere where you can use these things. As we speak, I'm having some items delivered to your home that will be more suitable for your stay."

Once again, I was speechless. The biggest smile spread across my face. She walked over and kissed me. Instantly, my "honeypot" got wet. She pulled away slowly.

She said, "Go Cherry, before you get yourself into trouble and miss your flight."

I opened my eyes from the kiss and realized, once again, that I was not dreaming. I grabbed my purse off the bed and headed for the elevator. Once inside, I thought about what she had just said, "... get myself into trouble." It was already too late for that. For some reason, I liked the sound or, maybe I should say, the feeling of trouble with her.

Although the plane ride only took a little over three hours, it felt like forever. I couldn't wait to get to Texas to see Grandma. I thought about calling her to let her know that I was coming home but decided against it. I wanted it to be a total surprise. I had spoken to William when I got to the airport. I told him that I was on my way home. He couldn't believe it.

He said, "What do you mean you're on your way home? Does that mean that you quit the internship? See, I told you family was more important. I love you so much, Cherry."

I couldn't believe how easy the words, "I love you" were for him to say to me, especially since he had a wife.

I said, "William, I didn't quit the internship. Your wife just had a change of heart, I guess. He interrupted, "Change of heart! Cherry, Lauren never has a change of heart when it comes to work. I've been with that woman for the majority of our lives and career decisions are things she's always, always sure about. So, what the hell got into her?"

I thought to myself, "Nothing got into 'her', but she was all up in 'me'."

I answered, "William, everything's fine. Like I said, she had a change of heart, I guess."

He said, "But that isn't Lauren at all."

With an attitude I said, "Instead of trying to figure out why she let me go home, can't you just be happy that I am going?"

He said, "Whoooaaaa, I think you're misunderstanding me. I'm happy. I guess I'm just shocked, too. Lauren never does stuff like this. Let me know when you arrive in Texas. I know your grandma will be thrilled to see you."

Grandma thought she was dreaming when she saw me on her doorsteps. We had the best time. Dr. Lauren stayed true to her word and made sure I had everything I needed when I arrived in Texas: yoga pants, jeans, sweats, hoodies, T-shirts, pajamas, underwear, sneakers, and slides. She made sure I had clothes that I could be comfortable in while at home, as well as outfits that I could wear when Grandma and I left the house.

I tried not to think of William and Dr. Lauren, or maybe I should say William or Dr. Lauren, but I couldn't help it, especially at night. For some reason, I stayed horny at night. Some nights, I would close my eyes and pretend Dr. Lauren was in bed with me. Other nights, I would close my eyes and pretend William was there. Either way, both made me feel good when I touched myself. What was scary was that I couldn't figure out whose touch I enjoyed more.

Oh, and it happened again! I thought I saw Braylen ride by the house several times.

By the time Spring Break came to an end, I was ready for a real break. I was exhausted because Grandma and I spent every minute together doing stuff– dinner dates, movies, shopping, walks, bowling, church, arts and crafts, cooking, gardening, miniature golf, and baking. I spent some time with Sterling and Greyson, too, but most of it was with Grandma.

CHAPTER
TWENTY-THREE

Turned Me Out

I arrived in Georgia on a Friday evening. I had received several calls from William and Dr. Lauren, each wanting to see me. I knew why William wanted to meet but was not quite sure about Dr. Lauren. I wasn't sure if it was business or something else. Part of me hoped it was strictly business—I didn't think I could handle a love triangle involving both a husband that I cared deeply for and his wife, with whom I had a professional relationship. Still, I couldn't deny that I missed the way Dr. Lauren made me feel. I weighed both options and decided to call Dr. Lauren first, hoping the conversation would stay focused on work, since my career goals were a main priority.

Dr. Lauren answered on the first ring. "Welcome back, Miss O'Brien. I assume you enjoyed Spring Break with your grandma. Now, it's back to business. I'll see you in the office in an hour." Click.

"Damn, well!," I said out loud.

"Maybe I should have called William first," I thought to myself.

So, I did. He answered on the first ring, too.

He said, "Hey, Cherry! I can't wait to see you. I've missed you so much."

I said, "I've missed you, too, William. But unfortunately, your wife has summoned, already."

He almost screamed through the phone, "You gotta be kidding me. I didn't even know she was back in town. Tell me you told her, no!"

I said, "She wants me in the office in an hour."

He said, "This is a joke, right?"

I said, "William, you know I don't have a choice."

He said, "Cherry, you always have a choice."

I did not feel like arguing with him.

I said, "You are right, so tomorrow, I will choose you!"

I arrived at the office within the hour, expecting everyone to be gone for the day. The place was buzzing with activity as if it were still regular hours. Several people were seated around the table. The projector was on, with notebooks and folders spread open. Pens, highlighters, and Post-it notes were scattered across the table. This meant we had a long night ahead.

By the time people started leaving the conference room, it was nearly midnight. Dr. Lauren and I left were the only ones left, and I was ready to go home. My feet ached, and my neck and back were tight from the plane ride; I was completely exhausted. I glanced at Dr. Lauren, who seemed to have plenty of energy left. I cleared my throat to get her attention, but she acted as if she hadn't heard me. So, I began clicking the top of my pen to make some noise.

Click. Click. Click. Click. Click. Click. Click. Click. Click. Click. Click. Click.

Finally, she looked at me over the top of her glasses. She took them off and cleared her throat.

She asked, "Is everything okay, Miss O'Brien?"

"How could this be the same woman who had just licked my "honeypot" less than a week ago?" I thought. I felt uncomfortable, and I wanted to get the hell out of there and go home.

I lied and said, "Yes, everything is fine. I'm just really tired from the plane ride, that's all."

She said, "Well, Miss O'Brien, you are a big girl, so I think you'll be just fine."

She readjusted her glasses. I couldn't believe the bitch. If looks could kill, she would be dead. I wanted to jump across the table and punch her in her damn face.

She removed her glasses, smiled, and said, "Unless there is something I can do to help you relax."

Did she mean what I thought she meant, I wondered.

With the voice of an innocent child, I asked, "Huh?"

She got up from her chair and started walking towards me.

In a flirtatious tone, she said, "I think you know exactly what I mean, Cherry."

Instantly, I was turned on. She pulled me out of my seat and kissed me. I felt weak.

I said between kisses, "We can't do this here. I mean … we can't do this anymore."

While unfastening my shirt, she said, "Are you sure about that? If you want me to stop, just say the word."

Instead of saying stop, I said, "But what if someone sees us?"

She unbuckled the snap on my pants, stuck her hands inside, and touched my spot.

She said, "Cherry, we are hundreds of feet off the ground. I don't think no one can see us. But if they can, let's stop talking and give them a show."

She slid my pants down and touched my spot again; then she removed my thong. I slid my shirt over my head. She unsnapped my bra. There I was, standing in my birthday suit. My breasts were standing erect, begging her to taste them. She just stood there, staring at me. I felt embarrassed, so I covered myself as best as I could with my arms. She giggled and started to undress herself. I looked at her absolutely perfect naked body. She was a goddess. We both stood looking at each other, completely naked. She came closer to me. I could feel my cheeks starting to burn. I don't know what got into me because instead of waiting for her to kiss me, I reached over and kissed her. I wanted her tongue in my mouth so bad. We stood on the floor while our tongues danced the tango. It was beautiful.

She motioned for me to get on the conference table. I obeyed. She spread my legs as far as they would go and just stared into my "honeypot". It felt like forever. I began to feel embarrassed again. I was about to close my legs, but she stopped me. She touched my clit with her finger. Her touch made me gasp, so she touched it again. I gasped again. She climbed on top of the table with me. She was so beautiful. She reached down and kissed me again. Then she began to suck on one of my breasts and massage my clit at the same time. The feeling was too much. The table was slick. I could feel myself inching up. Every move I made, she made it with me. Just when I was about to climax, she stuck her face into my "honeypot". She sucked, and licked, and nibbled, and pulled, and sucked, and licked, and nibbled, and pulled. I had reached the edge of the table, and my head hung off. She continued sucking, licking, pulling, and nibbling. I continued to slide up the table, trying to find something to grasp onto. The next thing I knew, I was balancing with my hands on the floor. All that remained on the table were my ass, my feet, and Dr. Lauren. With her face still planted in my "honeypot", she feasted like a hungry bear. My arms grew weak and began to shake. My body climaxed, and my arms gave out.

I woke up on the conference room floor, wrapped in a blanket, still completely naked. It was 3:15 in the morning. Dr. Lauren was sitting nearby in her office chair, also wrapped in a blanket, focused on laptop. When she noticed me stirring, she took off her glasses.

She looked at me and said, "I'm so glad you are awake; I just got hungry again."

She stood up and let her blanket fall. She joined me on the floor and started feasting.

CHAPTER
TWENTY-FOUR

Sexed Me

"**G**ot damn! This lady is too much," I thought to myself.

She wasn't just hungry; she was ravenous, and I was a six-course meal. By the time I left the office, I was utterly exhausted, barely able to summon the energy to drive home. When I inserted the key into the lock and stepped inside, I moved quietly, hoping not to wake Summer and Aubrey—I didn't have the energy to explain where I'd been or what I'd been doing. Not that it needed an explanation; the scent of sex clung to me.

I slipped off my shoes and tiptoed toward my bedroom. Once inside, I longed to collapse onto the bed, but I knew better. I needed a hot shower to wash away every sin I'd just committed.

I quickly showered. When I looked at myself in the mirror, I barely recognized the person staring back. I never imagined finding myself in a situation like this—or, more precisely, having sex with a woman. I questioned if it made me gay or bisexual. I didn't feel like I was either since I wasn't reciprocating physically. Yet, I couldn't deny that I enjoyed what she was doing to me. I kissed her, but that was as far as it went on my end. I silently thanked God she hadn't asked me for anything more, but I couldn't help wondering what would happen if she did. What then? I didn't have any desire to lick her back. Was that selfish of me?

"Maybe I should end this now before things go any further," I said loudly.

The thoughts were making my headache. I felt completely drained, starved, and dehydrated. I didn't even have the energy to put on my body butter. I slipped on my pajamas and tiptoed to the kitchen for a bottle of water and a pack of crackers. Once back in my room, I closed and locked the door, not wanting any disturbances. I pulled back the covers, opened the water bottle, and drank half of it in one gulp. I ate one cracker and finished the water. I glanced at the clock on my nightstand. It was 8:27. I crawled into bed, pulled the covers up to my chin, and promptly fell asleep.

CHAPTER
TWENTY-FIVE

Whipped Me

W hen I finally woke up, I felt better, but my body was sore as hell. I felt like I had just trained at the gym. If I had known what was going to happen next, I would not have gotten out of bed.

The was 3:07 p.m.

I checked my phone. I had missed several calls—from Momma, Grandma, my brothers, Dr. Lauren, and, of course, William. I began returning calls, starting with Grandma and Momma. Each conversation was essentially the same: "Yes, I made it back to Georgia safely. Sorry for not calling sooner. I went to work and ended up staying later than planned. When I got home, I went straight to sleep and slept longer than I intended."

I didn't bother to call Dr. Lauren. I had no intention of seeing her anymore that day.

Next, I called William. He answered the phone on the first ring.

"Cherry, is everything OK? I have been worried sick?"

I answered, "What do you mean? I'm completely fine. I slept most of the day. Lauren asked me…I mean Dr. Lauren…I mean your wife asked me to come to the office Friday. We stayed way longer than expected. When I finally got home Saturday morning, I showered then crashed."

He didn't say anything. His silence made me uncomfortable. He was quiet way longer than I wanted him to be.

I asked, "William, are you still there?"

Condescendingly, he replied, "I'm here, Cherry. How about dinner? With all this working and sleeping you have to be starving!"

To cut the tension, I said, "You're right, William. I'm starving, but not just for food. I can hardly wait to see you."

He simply responded, "See you soon, Cherry," and ended the call.

I quickly showered and dressed. William sounded sad and disappointed. I hurried to my car and drove straight to our spot. It only took me about forty-five minutes. When I pulled into the driveway, the front door opened instantly. William stepped out onto the porch and crossed his arms. I put the car into park. I had never seen that look on his face before. I opened the car door and stepped out. I smiled as I walked towards the house, hoping to change his mood. His expression was unchanged. He moved from blocking the door, so I could walk inside. His eyes softened a little. He pulled me into his arms. His embrace was warm, loving, and secure. I finally breathed. He released me, and we looked into each other's eyes.

Our eyes said everything that needed to be said.

We kissed. He lifted me off the floor. I wrapped my legs around his waist. I wore a dress without panties, on purpose. When he noticed, he moaned and grabbed my ass cheeks. He carried me to the bedroom. The bed was already pulled back. He placed me on it. I moved over, expecting him to join me.

Instead, he said, "Come back, Cherry, I want to look at you. Do you know how long it has been since I've laid eyes on you? Just let me look at you."

He stood there with the gentlest eyes.

He said, "Cherry, your beauty is so unique. I could stare at you forever."

I said, "Thank you, William, but I would rather you do something else to me."

As if it had a heartbeat, his dick jumped in his pants.

He said, "In that case, how about you get undressed for me."

I lifted my hips off and pulled my dress over my head. I wasn't wearing a bra either. Both of my nipples saluted William. He unbuttoned his shirt and removed it. He was absolutely gorgeous. His chest was smooth as butter. The hairs below his belly button was as fine as the hair on a baby's head. He unbuckled his belt and unbuttoned his slacks. They fell to the floor; then, he unleashed 'The Chocolate Anaconda'. I forgot how massive he was. My eyes grew. Its veins bulged. I moved over in the bed, so he could join me.

He said, "Come back, Cherry, I'm still looking at you."

I moved back to my original position. He did something I wasn't expecting. He grabbed "The Chocolate Anaconda" with both hands and started stroking it. Whenever he would reach the top, he would use his thumb to circle its head, while keeping his eyes on me. Pre-cum was oozing.

He said, "Cherry, spread your legs for me."

I quickly obliged, thinking he was ready to come inside. Instead, he continued stroking "The Chocolate Anaconda." That shit was turning me on. My "honeypot" was drenching the sheets underneath me. I wanted him to touch me, but he was too busy touching himself. So, I did what I had to do. I reached down and touched myself. My fingers knew exactly what to do. They learned that from Dr. Lauren. I spread my legs wider to get a better feel. My right hand was massaging my clit while my left hand was massaging my nipples. For a minute, I forgot William and "The Chocolate Anaconda" were in the room, but William quickly reminded me. I opened my eyes to the "The Chocolate Anaconda" singing.

William regained his composure. I was about to lose mine.

He said, "Control yourself, Cherry. Let me be the one to take you there."

Just the sound of his voice made my breathing increase. I wanted to explode.

He said, "Cherry, please."

At that moment, I had a vision. I tried to block it out, but it was too late. I was lying in bed with Dr. Lauren and William. All three of us in bed was too much. I began to shake. My "honeypot" overflowed. Finally, my breathing began to slow down. My eyes were still closed. I was too embarrassed to open them. My body finally relaxed. He rested both of my thighs in his massive arms and pulled me closer. Then, his soft, gentle lips kissed my clit. He gave it one tug, and I exploded again.

After that, we made love. William did not bust a quick nut. He did not have sex with me. He did not fuck me. He made love to me. He kissed me, rubbed me, caressed me, stroked me, licked me, and filled me with every inch of himself. It was slow then fast then slow again. He took his time with me and only sped up when I wanted him to. It was like he was inside of my head and knew exactly what I wanted and how I wanted it. Our bodies were in perfect sync. Our breathing and moaning were in sync. I knew it was love when tears from pure pleasure started flowing from my eyes. When he looked at me and noticed, he cried, too. It was like Heaven on Earth. I can't remember when the love-making ended. I just remember waking up to the smell of bacon coming from the kitchen. I rolled over and felt for William. He was not there, but I knew where to find him. I got out of bed and put on the robe that William had placed across the foot of the bed and headed towards the bathroom.

When I finally made it to the kitchen, William had a nice spread on the table: grits, bacon, waffles, chicken, eggs, juice, and fruit. The man was amazing. How could Dr. Lauren not see that? How could she not be head over heels for such a rare gem?

William noticed me and said, "Good morning, Beautiful!"

I blushed. "Good morning, William!" I responded. "How did you sleep?"

He said, "I didn't sleep much, but I must say I rested better than I have in weeks."

Again, I blushed.

He said, "I hope you are ready to eat! I need you to regain the weight that you've lost."

"So, you've noticed?" I said with a smile.

He replied, "Definitely!"

He didn't return a smile. Instead, I noticed him grinding his teeth.

Afterwards, all I wanted to do was crawl back in bed, watch TV, and snuggle in his arms. After about an hour or so, I could sense that something was wrong. The beating of his heart even felt different.

I said, "William, is everything OK?"

He said, "Cherry, I think we need to talk."

I am smart enough to know that when most people say, "we need to talk", something bad comes next. I sat up in bed so I could look at his eyes. I guess the look on my face told him that I expected the worst.

He said, "Cherry, you don't have to look so worried or upset. I have no intentions of saying or doing anything to upset you."

I said, "Just tell me what's wrong!'

He said, "Cherry, I was hoping that you would tell me what's wrong. You seem different- distant, distracted. Before you say it's just work, I know you better than that, or at least I thought I did, so be honest with me, Cherry. What is going on with you? We haven't talked as much. I can feel it in my gut. We have always been honest with each other, so let's not mess that up. You told me from the beginning how important honesty is to you and how a few important people in your life had not been honest with you, and the damage it did. Just tell me what's going on. Whatever it is, we can work through it. We can fix it. We just have to be honest with each other. Nothing you say or do will ever change how I feel about you. I hope you feel the same about me."

I felt stunned, embarrassed, and guilty. I could not hold back the tears. They started flowing. The guilt was eating at me so badly that I jumped out of the bed and started putting on my sweats as quickly as I could. William tried to stop me, and I pulled away from him.

He said, "Cherry, please stop! Just tell me what's wrong? What's going on? Whatever it is, we can fix it."

With tears and snot flowing, I screamed, "William, everything is not that simple. Some things can't be fixed."

In his calming voice, he said, "Well, in my world, Cherry, everything is that simple. It all starts with honesty and communication, and I am begging you for both."

I said, "William, just let me get my shit and get out of here!"

He took three steps back and got out of my way. I tossed my bag across my shoulder, grabbed my purse off the chair, and headed for the front door. William followed closely behind me. I put my hand on the doorknob.

I was just about to turn it when he said with a very shaky voice, "I'm begging you. Please don't walk out of my life. Whatever it is, I promise you we can work through it. I love you, Cherry. You complete me. You make me happy. I haven't been this happy in a long time. I can breathe because of you. I'm alive because of you. I'm healed because of you. I can smile because of you. Please, Cherry, just say it. Just tell me what is wrong. We can fix it. Nothing you say can destroy the love and respect I have for you."

I was crying even harder.

With more shame than I've ever felt before, I said, "William, I'm sleeping with your wife."

CHAPTER
TWENTY-SIX

Kept Me In The Dark

Willliam grabbed his chest and fell to his knees. I ran over to him.

I yelled, "OMG, William! Are you OK? God, please no! William, answer me! Willliamm!"

Through heavy breaths, while grabbing at his chest, he said, "Cherry, it hurts."

I started rambling through my purse for my cell phone.

I screamed, "William, I'm calling 911. I think you're having a heart attack."

I dialed the three digits, and his eyes closed. Soon, I heard sirens approaching. I ran to the door and opened it. I stepped onto the porch to hurry the paramedics into the house. William was conscious but barely. The paramedics started working on him. I was hysterical. One asked me what happened. I was too upset to get it out. Finally, William started mumbling.

Weakly, he said, "I…am…fine. I'm fine."

One paramedic responded, "Sir, we are preparing to take you to the hospital."

William repeated, "I'm…fine."

The other paramedic said, "Your vitals say differently, sir."

I interjected, "William, I think they're right. You should go with them."

The first paramedic said, "Please listen to your daughter, sir. We've seen situations like these before that are way more serious than people realize."

William said angrily, "For the last time, I am fine."

The paramedics started packing up. Right before walking out the door, they told William to follow up with his primary care physician as soon as possible. I closed and locked the door behind them. I joined William on the sofa.

I said, "William, I really think you should have gone—"

He interrupted me, "Tell me how long this has been going on!"

I asked, "What are you talking about?"

He screamed, "How long have you and Lauren been fucking, Cherry?"

The anger in his voice made me jump. I had forgotten that I had told him that.

I said, "William, we can talk about this later. I don't want you to get upset again."

He said, "Dammit, Cherry, just tell me!"

I lowered my head and said, "It all started last week in California. I'm so sorry, William."

William said something that I couldn't believe. Something that I was sure I totally heard wrong. Something that made me think I was about to need 911 next.

He said, "Cherry, you have nothing to be sorry about. This is all my fault. This has happened before, but I never thought it would happen again, especially not to you. I am so sorry. This is all my fault. Please forgive me."

I made my way to the wingback chair on the opposite side of the room. I felt confused. What in the hell was William talking about? What did he mean that it was all his fault? When and how did this happen before?

I looked at him.

He looked at me.

I looked angry.

He looked angry.

I looked hurt.

He looked hurt.

Finally, I asked, "William, what the fuck is going on?"

His answer shook me to the bones.

With regret in his voice, he began to explain.

"About eight years ago, Lauren's firm brought in a young, new hire named Amelia Ford. She was smart, hardworking, quick on her feet—everything the firm valued. Naturally, she and Lauren worked closely together. Amelia was stunning, with perfectly tanned skin, long, blond hair, and an athletic build. While her looks were striking, it was her intelligence that everyone admired; she played a key role in attracting major clients and high-profile deals for the company. She was well-liked by everyone. It turned out that Lauren liked her a little too much. They ended up having an affair."

Before William got to that last part, I already knew where the story was going. He got up from his chair and started towards me.

I stopped him and said, "Please don't. Just finish the story."

He continued, "The affair between Amelia and Lauren went on for almost a year. Of course, I had no idea because things were already not good between the two of us. One day, Amelia decided that she wanted things to end. Lauren was not having it. She started blackmailing Amelia. When Amelia had enough, she went to the one person she thought she could go to for help: me."

My eyes widened.

I questioned, "You?"

William continued, "Amelia told me that she and Lauren had been having an affair. Amelia had never been with a woman before, and she was completely head over heels. Over time, Lauren's controlling nature at work began to seep into their relationship. Lauren didn't want Amelia spending time with her friends or dating anyone else. She even discouraged her from being around her own family. Lauren started making Amelia work late hours just to keep tabs on her.

The pressure became so intense that it started affecting Amelia's performance at work. She begged Lauren to keep their relationship strictly professional, but Lauren wouldn't hear of it. She warned Amelia that if she tried to leave, she would destroy her career. At first, Amelia didn't take it seriously, but Lauren proved that she wasn't bluffing. She started deleting important files from Amelia's computer and changing her calendar appointments so that Amelia would arrive late. Some of the big clients Amelia had brought to the firm canceled their contracts without any explanation."

I couldn't believe what I was hearing.

"Amelia realized that Lauren had her right where she wanted her. This forced her to continue their relationship for several more months. During that time, Lauren discovered that Amelia was 'cheating on her' with a guy she had been dating. Lauren lost her fucking mind, to say the least."

This sounded like some shit from an obsessed lover movie. Was he talking about the same Lauren that I had gotten to know over the last few months; the same lady that I had been sleeping with?

William continued to talk, but I was not listening. I guess I got caught up in my own thoughts somewhere. However, I had to make myself focus on what he was saying.

"She started following Ameila's boyfriend around town. Things started happening to him. For instance, once he got run off the road by some 'lunatic driver.' Then, he was leaving work and all four of his tires were slashed. Again, another time, someone broke into his apartment and wrecked the place. They didn't steal anything, just wrecked the place. Amelia knew who to blame. Too afraid to go to the police for help, she came to me."

I looked at William with disbelief.

"That's when, Amelia told me everything. I was in total shock, but I did what any person in my situation would do. I helped the poor girl the only way I knew how."

I questioned, "What did you do William? Did you go to the police?"

He answered, "No, but, I probably should have. She would have said the relationship was consensual. Amelia would have definitely lost her job and possibly her career. Lauren wouldn't have admitted to any of the things she did to Amelia or her boyfriend. Hell, she probably didn't actually do any of the things to the boyfriend. She probably paid some flunkies do it. I apologized to Amelia for all the trouble Lauren had caused. Then, I gave her enough money to start a new life far away from my evil ass wife."

I jumped up from my chair because it was my turn to talk.

I said, "William, if you knew all of this, why would you introduce me to her? Why would you allow her the opportunity to do the same things? Did you set me up? Are you fucking insane?"

He interrupted, "Cherry, I would never do anything like that to any woman, especially to you. Please have a seat and let me continue."

I was boiling. I was furious, but I needed answers, and I needed them immediately. I sat down to give him the chance to attempt an explanation.

He started again. "After discovering all of this information, I was so upset with Lauren. I looked at her totally differently. I wanted to leave her. I wanted to take our son and run, but I couldn't because as much as I hated her, our son loved her. I had to think of a way to confront her with the information. I waited a few weeks to make sure Amelia had enough time to leave town. After that, I mailed an anonymous letter to our home detailing the ins and outs of Lauren and Amelia's relationship. I was sure to include everything that Lauren did to Amelia and her boyfriend. I pretended to be someone who was connected to the firm. When Lauren arrived home from work one evening, I was sitting in the living room reading the letter."

When she saw the look on my face, she knew something was wrong.

I looked at her with pure hatred and disgust. I said noth-ing. I just handed her the letter. At first, she denied it all, but of course I knew she was lying. She walked around for weeks like she was mad at the world, like the entire thing was a lie. She even found a way to twist it to make it my fault, which made me hate her even more."

He continued, "Then another 'package' arrived—this one sent directly to me. It included a letter and explicit photos of Lauren and Amelia together—naked, intimate, all of which I'd conveniently gotten from Amelia before she left town, knowing they might come in handy one day. To strengthen the story, I included a cassette tape of Amelia secretly recording Lauren—capturing the threats against Amelia's life, career, and even her boyfriend. The 'anonymous sender' claimed he'd go public with the evidence if he didn't receive money. Lauren broke down and confessed everything. She begged and pleaded with me not to leave her, promising it would never happen again.

We went through years of marriage counseling. Lauren claimed she'd been going through a mid-life crisis or even a mental breakdown, saying she didn't know what had come over her. She seemed genuinely remorseful."

Still not quite sure of what to say, I let him keep talking.

"After that, things between us were never the same, but not because I didn't want them to be. I tried, but I'm not sure if I ever got that same effort from her. She buried herself deeper into her work, and we drifted farther apart. If I am honest with you, Cherry, I started feeling sorry for her, and I blamed myself for what happened. I thought maybe I wasn't attentive enough. Maybe life was too stressful for her, being a full-time mother, wife, and having a full-time career. I wanted things to get better for Lauren. I saw so much good in her, or at least I thought. She was my everything- my college sweetheart, the love of my life, the mother of my son, my world. When I introduced y'all, I never thought she was capable of doing those things again. I thought she had really changed. Although our relationship was nothing like it used to be, I still saw the good in her. I still saw the person I thought she was when we met in college. If I thought for a minute that she would have done this to you, I would have never introduced you to her. In fact, I thought counseling had fixed or healed her. I'm sorry, Cherry, I had no idea."

There was nothing left to say. The tears were flowing like a river; tears of hurt, deception, anger, and regret. Hatred towards Dr. Lauren filled the room. It was so thick; we were blinded by it. We both wanted revenge, but I wanted it more, and that's exactly what I would get.

CHAPTER
TWENTY-SEVEN

Sickened Me

When I left William's place that night, I felt empty inside. I hated Dr. Lauren; a part of me hated him more. If it wasn't for him, none of this shit would have happened. How could he not think Dr. Lauren would do something like that again? Why would he even introduce me to her? Hell, he could have at least told me about her so my guard would be raised.

The drive back to my apartment seemed long, a lot longer than it had ever been. When I unlocked the door, I knew Summer and Aubrey would be up. I was kind of hoping they would be. when I stepped inside of our apartment, our eyes met. They immediately knew that I needed them. Summer made some warm cocoa. Aubrey grabbed a blanket, and we snuggled on the sofa. We sat there until I was finally ready to talk. I was so ashamed of the person I had become and some of the decisions I had made. I still couldn't be totally honest with them though even though I trusted them with my life. I told them that I had been dating an older man. Things were going really well. He had been showering me with the finer things in life, including the new car I was driving. I told them that the sex was amazing, mind-blowing even. Then, the lies started. I told them I got caught in a love triangle with him and his best friend. He found out about his best friend and me. Instead of being angry, he told me some things about his best friend that kind of scared me. He told me that his best friend was using me. He often mistreated women and his actions were criminal. I felt like a complete idiot. To make matters worse, his friend had done the same thing to another girl. Threats were made, and she was forced to leave town.

My words made their eyes grow big. They were scared, so I stopped talking.

Summer spoke first. "Riri, how did you meet this friend of your boyfriend?"

Without thinking, I said, "I work with him."

Summer said, "Are you serious? Riri, you need to tell Dr. Lauren immediately. Maybe she can help by filing an official report or something, especially since he has done this before."

I shouted, "I wouldn't dare tell her!"

Summer said, "I'm sorry, Riri, I'm just saying. You don't have to."

I said, "Summer, I didn't mean to yell at you. I'm just a little freaked out, that's all."

Aubrey said, "Well, Riri, do we need to call the police?"

I said, "No, Aubrey, the last thing I want to do is get the police involved."

She said, "What do you mean? This man sounds dangerous. What if he does something to you? Riri, we have to take
these kinds of things seriously!"

I replied, "Believe me, I'm taking this very seriously. I can
this handled."

Aubrey continued, "Riri, we are here for you. We want to
make sure you're thinking clearly and about your safety."

I sighed heavily and rested my head in the palm of my
hands. To be honest, I couldn't believe that shit was happening to me.

"Dr. Lauren messed with the wrong one this time," I
thought to myself, "and I was going to make her pay."

I got up from the sofa and said, "I have a really bad headache, and I'm too tired to talk about this anymore. I need to
lie down."

"No, wait," Aubrey protested, "we have to figure this out."

I said, "Y'all, I can't do this right now. I really need to lie
down. The room is spinning, and I feel sick and dizzy."

Each of them took one of my arms and guided me to my
bedroom. They helped me out of my clothes, pinned my hair
into a bun, and turned on the shower. Even if I'd wanted to
protest, I didn't have the strength, mentally, emotionally, or
physically.

They turned off the water and helped me to dry off. When
the water shut off, they helped me out, drying me off with
a towel. Summer slipped a T-shirt over my head while Aubrey turned down the bed covers. I climbed into bed, and they
curled up beside me. We stayed that way until morning.

When I woke up Monday morning, I had no intention
of getting out of bed. I pulled the covers over my head when
daylight invaded my room. I could hear Summer and Aubrey

moving around. Every so often, they would open my door to check on me. When night fell, the same routine occurred, shower, then they curled up in bed with me. This went on for three days. I knew I needed to stop feeling sorry for myself. My actions were affecting them. Not only was I messing with my future, but I was also messing with theirs. Me not getting out of bed and leaving the apartment meant them not leaving the apartment and them not going to class or work, I could not continue to let that happen. The next morning, I moved differently.

I got out of bed at four that morning.

Sleepily, Summer asked, "Riri, are you OK? What are you doing?"

I said, "I'm getting ready for work, and the two of you need to do the same."

She said, "Riri, we don't have to do this today. We need to make sure things are safe before we go out."

At that moment, I realized that they were afraid. Afraid something was going to happen to me or even them. That's why they were sticking around, to protect me.

How could I do that to them? How could I cause them to worry and live in fear? I felt awful!

I put on my game face and said, "Guys, I'm fine. Trust me. I'm not afraid of anything and neither should you. I have this handled."

They looked at each other with so much uncertainty.

I sat on the edge of the bed.

I said, "Summer and Aubrey, trust me. I can handle this, and if I couldn't, I would tell you. You have absolutely nothing to worry about or no reason to sit around here. I don't need protection."

They gave me a look that told me that I was not convincing them.

I said, "Look, y'all can stay here if you want to, but I'm getting dressed then heading out the door."

I went into the bathroom and closed the door. By the time I'd showered and returned to my bedroom, it was empty. I sat on the edge of my bed and pulled my phone out of my purse, only to find it completely dead. I plugged it in to charge and continued getting dressed. An hour later, I headed to the kitchen for breakfast. Summer and Aubrey must have known I'd be hungry—they'd already made bacon, waffles, eggs, and freshly-squeezed orange juice. We sat together at the breakfast table. They tried to keep the conversation light, but I could tell that the discussion from four days ago was still weighing on them. I pretended not to notice and mentioned that I'd probably be home late that night since I hadn't been to work all week. They didn't like that, but I reassured them I was fine because secretly I was plotting my revenge.

I grabbed my phone and my purse and headed out the door. When I got to my car, I paused for a moment. It felt like my heart was about to jump out of my chest. My breathing increased. I felt like I was about to pass out.

"I really think I'm having a heart attack," I thought to myself.

I dropped my cell phone then grabbed my chest.

I closed my eyes. I was scared. I found myself doing what any sane person would do at a time like that: I cried out to God for help and forgiveness.

With tears running down my face, I did what Momma, Daddy, and Grandma taught me to do. I prayed. "Heavenly Father, I come before You with a heavy heart and a restless spirit. Lord, I need Your help and guidance. My heart is racing, and I feel overwhelmed by the battle ahead of me. Please calm my anxious mind and fill me with Your peace that surpasses all understanding.

Father, I ask for Your forgiveness for my sins. Cleanse me, Lord, and make me whole. I know I fall short, but Your grace is sufficient, and Your mercy is everlasting. Help me to walk in Your ways and to trust in Your perfect plan for my life.

I am crying out to You, Lord, because I cannot do this alone. Be my strength when I am weak. Be my wisdom when I am uncertain. Guide my steps and give me the courage to face the challenges before me with faith and resilience.

Wrap me in Your love, Lord, and remind me that You are always with me. Help me to surrender my fears and worries to You, trusting that You will fight this battle for me and lead me to victory according to Your will.

Thank You, Father, for hearing my prayer. I trust in You, and I place my hope in Your unfailing promises. In Jesus' name, I pray. Amen."

I felt myself beginning to calm down. My breathing steadied, and the tightness in my chest eased. As I sat in the car, trying to regain control, my phone started ringing. I fumbled around on the floor for it and checked the caller ID—it was none other than Dr. Lauren. I let it go to voicemail; after everything I'd just gone through, I definitely wasn't ready to speak with her.

I noticed then that I had numerous unread texts and a full voicemail. I listened to the messages first; everyone was from William or Dr. Lauren. I was starting to think the two of them deserved each other. Moving on to the texts, it was the same—messages from William and Dr. Lauren. William was concerned, asking if I was okay and pleading with me to call him. Dr. Lauren, on a professional note, wanted to know why I hadn't shown up for work. Personally, she asked if I was alright and what was going on.

"Fuck y'all," I thought to myself.

I started my car, put it in drive, then sped out of the parking lot. At what felt like the speed of light, I arrived at work. Again, my breathing started to increase, and my heart started to pound. I grabbed the steering wheel with my right hand and let down the window with my left one. The breeze that rushed through the car helped me to calm down. I sat in my car for fifteen more minutes.

I pulled down the visor, looked at myself in the mirror and said, "Get it together, Riri! You can't let her control you like this. Don't be afraid to face your giant!"

I turned on the radio to get my mind right. The perfect song began to play through the speakers– "I Told the Storm". The lyrics ministered to my soul, especially those that talked about no weapons forming will prosper and I'm more than a conqueror.

I got my confirmation. I prepared myself and exited my vehicle. When I stepped into the office, I could tell that my absence had been noticed; everyone was looking at me as if they had seen a ghost. Their eyes were glued to me as I got on the elevator. It was time for me to do the inevitable: go see the boss. When I got to her office door, my first instinct was to knock, but I decided to make a bolder entrance. I just walked in.

That was a big mistake!

I walked into a meeting with some people I had never seen before; I assumed they were future investors. I must have scared everyone in the room, especially Dr. Lauren, because she dropped everything in her hands. Her eyes widened and her mouth flew open.

I said, "Umm, excuse me for interrupting. I didn't realize there was a meeting in progress. I can, um, come, um, back later."

Dr. Lauren said, "No apology is needed, Miss O'Brien. The meeting's just ending."

She turned her attention to the men in the room. "Gentleman, I will have Miss O'Brien email all the details. I will get back to you in a few days."

She walked to the door and stood by it signaling that the meeting was over.

CHAPTER
TWENTY-EIGHT

Ignited Me

She closed the door behind her, and the questions started.

"Cherry, where have you been? Are you OK? Do you know how worried I've been? If one more day had passed without hearing from you, I was planning to come to your home to check on you!"

"Sounds like someone else I know. Hell, maybe they are more alike than I realized," I thought to myself.

Finally, I spoke, "Sorry, Dr. Lauren. I've been feeling awful these last few days. In fact, I was in the hospital with the flu and a stomach bug. I got dehydrated. It was awful. I left my apartment by ambulance. I was too sick to call anyone. I was totally out of it. I finally got released from the hospital yesterday. I knew, at that point, a phone call or email wouldn't suffice. I wanted to explain everything face to face. Please don't fire me. I promise I won't let anything like this happen again. I'm so sorry."

I couldn't believe how easily the lies just rolled off my tongue.

She ran over to me and gave me a hug.

"OMG, Cherry," she cried, "I had no idea. I'm so sorry. I figured it had to be bad. I was worried sick about you. How are you feeling now? Do you need anything? Sit down. Have you eaten today?"

I pretended to hug her back while inaudibly saying, "Dumb bitch!"

I said, "No, I feel much better now. The hospital staff did an amazing job taking care of me. In addition, my roommates never left my side."

To make the lie seem even more believable, I added, "Once Grandma found out that I was sick, she hopped on the first plane and flew to Georgia. I dropped her off at the airport on my way to work this morning."

"Oh goodness, Cherry," Dr. Lauren exclaimed. "I'm so glad you're OK. I was worried sick about you, and now I see I had every right to be concerned. You believe the thoughts I was having. Cherry, I care about you. Go home. You need your rest. You have no business back in the office this soon."

"Did this bitch just say she cared about me?" I thought. "What the fuck???"

"No, I don't want to go home. I need to be here," I said.

"Ok," she said, "if you insist, but we'll definitely take it slow. How about we start with the clients that just left my office?"

We got straight to work.

"Damn, it didn't take much convincing her ass at all," I thought.

THE NEXT FEW MONTHS FLEW BY. MY LAST SEMESTER OF COLlege was coming to an end, which meant so was my internship. I can honestly say during that time I had accomplished so much. I had learned a lot about the engineering business and corporate America. Although I despised Dr. Lauren as a person, I had to admit that she was an amazing businessperson and mentor. She ran every aspect of the company. She was the face of the company. Her name carried weight. She brought millions of dollars into the company each year. On the professional side of things, I was truly blessed to have had the opportunity to work under her. Because we also had a personal relationship, she taught me everything she knew. There was no doubt in my mind I, too, would flourish in the engineering field. The best part was I had already gotten accepted into graduate school in California, and I would be working with a large engineering firm out there.

As far as my love triangle went, things were going as planned but getting a little difficult to manage, if that makes sense. After my fake sickness, Dr. Lauren had become overprotective. She was always checking on me. If she didn't hear from me, then she became overly concerned. It was almost like having another grandma. William, on the other hand, made sure I spent as much time with him as possible. He knew I was still seeing Dr. Lauren, and he heavily disagreed. But I explained that I needed to break things off with her slowly so she would not mess up my future with the other firm in California. Nevertheless, the thought of us being together infuriated him, so he made sure that I had little time alone with her. This made Dr. Lauren suspicious. A little too suspicious. She questioned me often and requested that I work over during the weekdays and come into the office on weekends. A few times she asked if I was seeing someone. I assured her that I wasn't, but she did not believe me. One day, I found her going through my purse. She claimed to be looking for a piece of gum, but I knew that was a lie because I was not a gum chewer. She was looking for the one item I always kept in it: my phone. From that moment forward, I made sure to delete any calls or texts between William and me.

"Nosey Bitch," I thought to myself.

I felt like I was being yanked between the both of them. Both were secretly doing things to prevent me from seeing the other. Of course, one knew about the other and the other didn't.

The sex with William and Dr. Lauren was incredible even though the thought of her made me sick to my stomach. Hey, a girl had to do what a girl had to do until it was time to get the bitch. So, I made sure that I learned everything I could from her.

The first Wednesday in May was my last day at the firm. Everyone had come together to give me a going away party. We drank champagne, ate cake, and opened gifts. It was really nice, and I must say I was going to genuinely miss everyone, except for one person, of course. When it was over, everyone insisted that I leave instead of helping tidy up, which made my plot for revenge so much easier. I got on the elevator and exited the building. I got in my car, drove around the corner, and parked. After that, I snuck back to the building and waited. I knew Dr. Lauren like the back of my hand. She wouldn't leave with everyone else. She was too much of a workaholic. I made sure everyone had left the building. I went back inside. I didn't bother to use the elevator. I took the stairs, careful to stay out of the view of the cameras. I snuck into Dr. Lauren's office and caught her off guard.

She said, "Cherry, you scared the shit out of me. I thought everyone had left for the night."

Then she smiled and said, "I get it. You came back for dessert."

She started walking towards me while kicking off her shoes and unbuttoning her shirt. She got closer and kissed my lips. My body tensed.

She said, "Don't act shy. We both know what you came back for."

Her words ignited me.

I said, "You're wrong, bitch. You have no idea why I'm here."

She pulled away and looked at me. By that time, the tears were already flowing.

She said, "Cherry, what's wrong? Sit down. What's going on!"

Shakily I said, "Dr. Lauren, you are what's wrong. I trusted you just like I trusted others in past. You did the same thing they did to me."

She had a confused look on her face.

I continued, "You lied to me! You manipulated me into believing that you were a good person. Yeah, bitch! I fell for all your lies. I even believed you when you told me I was special."

She interrupted, "Cherry, what are you talking about? You are spe–"

I screamed, "Don't interrupt me! Let me finish!"

I think I scared her a little because she fell down into her office chair.

Through sobs, I continued, "You told me that I was special, that you hadn't done anything like this since college. But you lied."

I had to pause to gather myself. She was looking at me like a deer in headlights.

"Don't look at me like that. You showed me a side of you that I didn't know existed. You spoke to me and touched me like I mattered to you. You made me feel beautiful. You wined and dined me. You taught me so much about this business. You told me that you would never hurt me. You even told me that you cared for me. All this time, you've been lying to me. You are one despicable human being. You did the same thing to me that you did to Amelia Ford."

The sound of Amelia's name sent fire through her body. She jumped up out of her seat and pounded her fist on the table.

Through clenched teeth she said, "How dare you? Don't you ever mention that name to me again. Little girl, you are way out of your league. You don't know who you are fucking with, and you certainly don't know what I am capable of. I don't know if this is some sort of game that you and that bitch Amelia are playing, but I can assure you that you both are mistaken if you think you can outsmart me. I'm the motherfucking boss around here and you two are nothing. Get the fuck out of my office. You are nothing in this business without me, and you never will be. Get the fuck out and close the fucking door behind you."

I was fuming.

I said, "Well, Dr. Lauren, evidently the game changed, and you didn't get the fucking memo. You may be the motherfucking boss, but I'm the motherfucking queen. The motherfucking queen that will the motherfucking game. While you were busy fucking me these few months, I've been busy making my moves. Let's just say that you shouldn't have mixed business with pleasure. I guess you haven't noticed that your financial records are really fucked up. It appears that 'someone' has been stealing money from the company, so, so much for your reputation in this business. You'll never be able to find that money, but I know someone who will be sitting pretty for a very long time, if you catch my drift. Second, you can't stop my future. My job is already secured in California, thanks to the 'superior recommendation' you gave to one of the largest engineering firms in the world. Third, oh, you may want to sit down for this one. I have been fucking your husband for over a year. Oh, and what a good fuck he is. All the things you hate about William, I love. Especially the way he makes me cum time after time after time. And to think, all those times you asked me if I was seeing someone. It was the very ma sleeping in the bed with you. I can't believe you never smelled me on him. I always made sure to give it to him good before I sent him home to you."

If looks could kill, I would have died at that moment.

She shouted, "You fucking bitch! Get the fuck out. This is far from over. Maybe I'll pay your sweet grandma a visit, or that little sister of yours that is a spitting image of you. What's her name? Oh, Lavender, that's it?"

At the mention of Grandma and Lavender, something reignited inside of me. I reached inside of my coat pocket, pulled out a gun, and shot her. She froze, looked down at her stomach, and grabbed it. She fell to the floor. I walked over to her and stood over her bleeding body. Our eyes met.

I shot her again, and again, and again.

Finally, her eyes closed. I slid the gun back into my coat, pulled my hood over my head and exited the building, careful to stay out of the camera's view. I walked back around the corner to my car. As I drove away, I could hear sirens in the distance.

CHAPTER
TWENTY-NINE

Calmed Me

I t was all over the news. A passerby heard shots and called 911. Someone had broken into the engineering firm. Evidently, the criminal did not expect anyone to be in the building. The building was searched, and Dr. Lauren's lifeless body was found. She had been shot multiple times. By the time the paramedics arrived, she barely had a pulse. She was rushed to the hospital and taken straight into surgery. She was in the ICU. There were no leads on the case.

The cameras captured nothing.

No suspects.

No witnesses.

Nothing.

The firm was devastated. William and Landon were devastated.

After that, I did not see much of William. He did not attend the university's graduation ceremony. He did call every day to let me know how things were going with Dr. Lauren. No improvement whatsoever.

"Thank God," I thought to myself.

Time was moving slow for William, Landon, and Dr. Lauren. Time was moving fast for me. After graduation, I moved to California in preparation for graduate school and my new job. Things were going great. I had an exquisite apartment thanks to all the money "Dr. Lauren had embezzled from the company". I was living my best life, but I missed William. I missed his touch. I missed his kisses. I missed our conversations. I missed "The Chocolate Anaconda".

He refused to leave Dr. Lauren and Landon's side. I became a little jealous. I wanted him in California with me. He made promises that I knew he couldn't keep. Our phone calls became almost nonexistent.

About five months later, my phone rang. I looked at the caller ID and answered.

"Hey stranger!"

The person on the other end said, "Hi, Cherry, I have some really bad news."

My heart started racing. I could barely breathe.

He continued in a broken tone, "It's Lauren! The doctors still aren't seeing much improvement. We're going to have to make some hard decisions soon. The detectives still have no leads. I can't believe this has happened. What kind of evil person could do such a thing? Don't get me wrong, Cherry, I know Lauren isn't perfect, but she didn't deserve this. No one does."

I wanted to interrupt him so badly to say, "Oh, the bitch deserved it all and more," but I didn't.

He continued. "I just don't know what to do. I'm hurting, and to see how bad our son is hurting is simply unbearable."

I stopped listening to him.

D R. SARTORI WAS LOOKING PALE AS HELL.

I said, "Dr. Satori, it was at this point in my life that I knew something was wrong with me."

I made air quotes when I said the "wrong with me part."

"I felt no remorse for what I did. I think I hated the bitch even more for not dying. I started to hate William for acting like he was so concerned and in love with her. Yeah, I know that's his wife and all, but how could he forget about all the pain she put him through, the pain she put Ameila Ford and her boyfriend through, or even the pain she could have caused me. But like I was saying, I knew something was wrong because I wasn't the least bit nervous or regretful about almost taking the life of another person. I wasn't nervous about possibly getting caught or anything like that. In fact, for the first time in my entire twenty something years of living, I felt at total peace. The entire situation actually calmed me and that led to a long line of lies, deceit, crime, and more."

CHAPTER
THIRTY

Reset Me

I stopped talking. I looked at Dr. Sartori. I mean, I really looked at her. She was pale as hell.

I asked, "Are you OK?"

Dr. Sartori said, "Dr. O'Brien, I have to admit. I didn't expect to hear any of this. In fact, in all of my years in business, I have never had anyone confess to attempted murder. I have to be honest with you, I don't think we will be able to continue this conversation any further because I'm quite uncomfortable. Although I agreed to patient-client confidentiality, there are lines that I dare not cross. Therefore, I don't think I can, in good conscience, continue with this session."

I jumped up out of my seat before I had a chance to think. It was like the "old Cherry", the one I had tried so hard to run away from and suppress, had reappeared.

I walked over from behind my desk, put one hand on each arm of her chair, leaned in until our noses practically touched, and said between clenched teeth, "Do you know how hard it was for me to get to this point, a point where I could even talk about this stuff? It took fucking years. I have never had the courage to share any of these things with anyone, Grandma, my brothers or sisters, my parents, my husband, or Summer and Aubrey. Now that I've opened up to you, there's no way in hell I'm going to let you walk out on me. Do your fucking job, the one I am paying you good fucking money to do. You knew you weren't coming in here to hear the story of *Cinderella*, so you will listen. You will let me finish, and you will not utter a word of this to anyone? Are we clear?"

The look on her face was one of pure horror. I felt ashamed. I backed up. I ran into the bathroom, and I looked at myself in the mirror. I saw the person that I tried to hide from everyone, the person I wanted to bury, the person that I swore to never become again. The tears started flowing. I cried an uncontrollable cry, one from deep down inside. I shook! I moaned! I cried out loud! The room began to spin.

I fell to the floor. I guess Dr. Sartori heard me, because she knocked on the door.

She said, "Cherry?"

She called me by my first name.

She continued, "Can I please come in?"

She didn't wait for me to answer.

"Cherry, are you OK?"

She sat on the bathroom floor next to me. She embraced me. I buried my face into her chest. I cried. She didn't say anything. She knew no words were needed. After about ten minutes, she stood up. She reached out her hand. I took it.

She pulled me to my feet. She turned on the faucet and wet one of the face towels folded in the cabinet. She gave it to me to wash my face.

After I was all cleaned up, she said, "Let's go back to your office to finish our conversation."

I looked over at her and said, "Ok, cool, but give me a minute if you don't mind."

She said, "Come out whenever you're ready."

She exited.

When I was sure she was away from the door, I was able to breathe again. I looked at myself in the mirror once more. I looked different. I felt different. I felt more in control. But, I knew things were going to have to be different once I stepped the door. I knew that Dr. Sartori was not "The One". My research for the right therapist failed me. I had only given her a glimpse of what was yet to come. She definitely wasn't ready for the rest of my confessions. She couldn't handle the things that I'd done since moving to California to get to where I am today. She wouldn't believe some of the people I've fucked, manipulated, embezzled from, blackmailed, blackballed, kidnapped, assaulted, humiliated, bribed, and lied to.

Where am I today? I'm exactly where I want to be in life. I own one of the largest engineering firms in the world. I have a beautiful home, fancy cars, a private jet, four beautiful children, a yacht, and vacation homes.

I'm married to the man of my dreams, maybe the only man I have truly loved and fully trusted.

But, none of that material shit means nothing when you are scared to close your eyes at night because of the visions and nightmares.

I looked in the mirror and said, "Cherry, you have survived too many storms to be bothered by raindrops."

This gave me the assurance that I needed.

I mumbled under my breath, "I told Dr. Santori when she first arrived that if I started my story and didn't finish it, there's no telling what I would do."

Now, I have to make sure Dr. Sartori never repeats anything I've said to her. I can't take any chances. I reached in the cabinet and felt under the stack of folded face towels. The cold, shiny, sharp object pricked my finger.

"Ouch," I grimaced, as I jerked back my finger.

A tiny bit of blood oozed out. I put my finger in my mouth to suck the blood. Carefully, I slid my hand back into the cabinet, careful not to get stabbed again. I grabbed the shiny object and slid it into the waist of my skirt. Then, I slightly tugged at my Tom Ford short, peplum jacket, and opened the bathroom door. What I was about to do was all her fault, because she ***reset me***!